Master
of the Jinn

A Sufi Novel

by
Irving Karchmar

Bay Street Press
Sag Harbor, NY

For information contact:
Bay Street Press, PO Box 725, Sag Harbor, NY 11963
Or contact the author at: Irvingk1945@gmail.com
http://www.masterofthejinn.com

ISBN: 1-59457-723-4

Library of Congress Catalog Card Number: 2004111692

Cover and interior design by Elana Kohn Spieth

Cover and Interior illustrations by Nadya Orlova

Printed in the United States of America

Dedicated to Dr. Javad Nurbakhsh,
Master of the Nimatullahi Sufi Order.

Master
of the Jinn

Contents

Prologue

In the name of *Allah*, the Merciful, the Compassionate.

I, Ishaq, named the scribe, am commanded by my Master to set forth the tale of the journey, from which, by the Mercy of God, I alone of my companions have returned.

Ali and Rami are no more. I saw them enter the fire. And Jasus also, that diviner of hearts, leaped into the flames. What became of the Hebrew sage and his daughter, or of the great Captain, I do not know. They would not leave when I bid them go.

But of this I am certain: The demon waits there still.

Baalzeboul—Lord of the *Jinn*.

Master of the Jinn

We show them the signs,
on the horizons and in themselves.
—The Koran, XLI: 53

At the first light of dawn over the middle desert, the black scarab-beetles come out of the sand and scurry up the face of the dunes to pray. Standing in line after endless line along ridge and crest, they face the rising sun and bow, as if in the prostration of obeisance, lifting their hindquarters to the warmth, gathering the morning dew of the cool desert night into droplets of water that role down the hard shell into the waiting mouth.

I wept at the sight of them. My last tears.

Here is a living mirror of the Merciful, I thought, *prayer that is answered each morning with the sustenance of life.* Would that my own heart reflected such devotion, that such unguarded surety filled my own breast instead of this wary beat that is man's lot; this accursed confluence of doubt and desire. Even wonders beyond measure devolve into worldly reason as the mind seeks desperately its own level, its diminishing order.

Rightly did the Master command these words. Well he knew both my doubt and my desire. Even at the beginning, on that day now long ago, each was evident to that unclouded eye.

I had walked all night again without water, bearing west and north across the *erg*, the great sand sea of the *Tenere*, hoping to cut the road that led to Agadez. My strength was nearly spent. Three hours before first light I fell exhausted beside the slipface of a small, crescent-shaped dune, half-digging into the *barchan* to find

10

what warmth I could against the desert night.

The wind had eased and I could see the stars in the moonless sky. Strangely I felt no fear, though I knew I could not live another day. My mind was calm and clear and distant as the stars. The desperation and sorrow that had overwhelmed me was nearly spent, ebbed away with my body's moisture, lost in the days and nights of my wandering. I could not explain it. Perhaps I had been given some small measure of *sakina*, that tranquility of heart that comes only with submission to the will of *Allah*, or perhaps I was mad, delirious from sun and thirst, but as my eyes closed I feared neither snake nor scorpion, nor any wild beast, nor death. Empty and dreamless, I drifted without thought or knowledge into dawn.

When the light woke me I thought for a moment that I was still dreaming. My dulled consciousness could barely comprehend the beetles suddenly rising around me, swarming like huge black spots before my startled eyes. I had never seen the like of them, and my first thought was that they had come to devour me. I quickly pulled myself out of the sand and crawled away, but to my surprise they regarded me not at all, hurrying up the dunes to form their lines toward the sun, called by that most ancient of *muezzins* to prayer.

Tears welled in my eyes as I saw the first droplets of water roll down their carapaces in answer, and so I struggled my own aching shell to kneel toward the dawn, and touched my own forehead to the sand.

The Tuaregs came upon me then, even as I invoked the All Merciful; advancing toward me in answer no less swift than to my insect brothers. Like spectres they came, riding slowly, suspicion narrowing their eyes above veiled faces; uncertain whether they

11

had come upon a madman in the sand or a demon.

They had been following the old salt trail west, guided by the star they call *Hajuj*, and surely had never found any more unlikely game on a morning's hunt. I shook my head when they made warding signs at me, but remained silent when they spoke. I could only understand a few words of *Tamashek*, their language, though I also wore a blue *gandura* robe, and so not knowing what to make of me they led me to their caravan's encampment.

There I was given water from a leather flask as we waited for their *modougou,* their caravan boss, to return. And I thanked the Almighty with every sip, and with every breath I praised Him for my deliverance. Slowly I felt a little better. After some time, the *modougou* rode in. He wore a long broadsword in a red scabbard and a black turban wrapped to veil all but his eyes; yet by his eyes I knew him. It was Afarnou.

We have met before, Afarnou and I.

"Pah!" he exclaimed, without dismounting. "I had given you all up for dead by now. Where are the others?"

He spoke French well and Arabic badly, but when I did not answer to either he dismounted and looked at me more closely. What he saw I could only guess, for he then explained slowly, as if to one gone simple-minded, that his camels were heavily laden with cones of salt from the mines at Tisemt and bound for Damergu in Niger to be exchanged for millet. Yet he would grudgingly spare one man and two camels to bring me to his father, the *Amenukal* of the noble people.

A camel litter was prepared and, without farewell, my guide and I crossed the *Tenere*. In two days we were in Agadez, and here I am still, tended by the *Amenukal's* wife and an elderly woman servant in a small room of their modest home.

The *Amenukal*, I have learned, wields authority over three tribes of the *Kel Ahaggar* in a loose federation, and is also the *amrar*, the 'Drum Chief' of his own tribe. What better symbol of a chief's authority among the once war-like Tuareg. But that was long ago. The years of French occupation had changed nearly everything of the old ways.

In courtesy, the *Amenukal* wears his small kingdom as if it were a robe of honor. He is an old man of impeccable hospitality and courtly manners, who carries himself with such quiet dignity that it ennobles the household.

He stood by my bedside and considered me gravely, but asked no questions at my condition, taking the note I had written without comment. Perhaps I am not the first fool to be found wandering in the desert, or perhaps he expects some reward, but he is a kind and generous host nonetheless, following the Arab admonition, *"Do good, and do not speak of it, and assuredly thy kindness will be recompensed thee."*

The two women, however, sit each day by the door outside my room, their whispers full of concern and uncertainty, wondering if I have been struck dumb by hardship and desert sun, or sorcery; whether I am addled or cursed.

Well might they wonder.

Now my pens are before me, and white paper and ink. The body is restored, yet the silence continues. I have not spoken since fleeing into the desert, mute to all now save the scribe's trust. Useless are any words but the full telling of the tale.

Allah grant me clear memory.

The Master

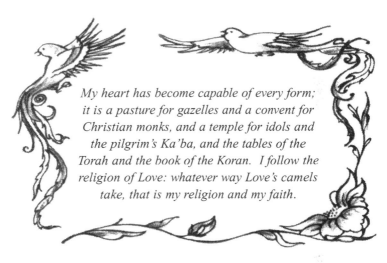

*My heart has become capable of every form;
it is a pasture for gazelles and a convent for
Christian monks, and a temple for idols and
the pilgrim's Ka'ba, and the tables of the
Torah and the book of the Koran. I follow the
religion of Love: whatever way Love's camels
take, that is my religion and my faith.*

—the *Tarjuman al-Ashwaq*
(The Interpreter of Desires)
by Muhyi'ddin Ibn al-Arabi

Master of the Jinn

> *With the vision of the soul,*
> *we witness*
> *The vision of God*
> *in the panorama of the heart*
> —the *Tarjiband* of Nur 'Ali Shah

We rise early in my Master's house, in that cool hour when the stars fade and gentle night is gathered into day. Do you know it? Silent is the house of the heart then. The tablet of the soul is washed clean.

In that hour I would sit by the window that overlooked the garden and down the hill to the fields and the city beyond. Ah, Jerusalem! It was midsummer, and the wind smelled of jasmine and the sea.

On that day I heard the familiar cry of a rooster crowing his greeting to the morning, but it was a dawn unlike any other in my life. Suddenly all the birds in creation seemed to join in the song; the trees of the garden were alive with larks and finches, canaries and turtledoves and a hundred others I could not name, each with its distinctive call; trill and chirp, caw and whistle.

I had never known them to gather so, nor to sing in such chorus; even nightingales were among them, which sing their songs only by the light of the stars. What instinct had brought them together I could not guess, but my solitude was broken. I retreated downstairs to heat water for the morning tea.

When kettle was set over flame, I opened the door facing the garden, thinking to end the serenade with an offering of bread-crumbs. There, to my surprise, was the Master, sitting on a small stone bench set among the trees.

I shook my head that he would choose to sit amid such a clamor and was about to ask if he would like a glass of tea, but at the sight of me he sighed and closed his eyes. Immediately the birds became silent, all of them at once, as if they had been singing for his ears alone.

I held my breath at the sudden stillness. Here was one of those small mysteries that are said to occur in the company of the Master. I had never been witness to one and the strange scene held me in awe.

How little I knew of such things then, or of the Master. My mind was filled with a hundred imaginings, but I could not explain the strange way of the birds. I did not know their song, nor understand their silence.

And there was no time to consider it further. The day had begun and the rest of the household soon appeared. I made no mention of the birds, and did not ask what the others might have seen or heard. The Master's ways are not to be discussed. Those in charge of the kitchen spread the *sufreh*, the long white tablecloth, over the Persian rugs covering the floor of the common room, then set out salt and bread, cheese and butter and jam for the morning meal. But I had little appetite for bread.

The Master did not come in to eat with us. When I looked into the garden sometime later he was nowhere to be seen, and the birds had vanished.

Not until early afternoon did the Master reappear. No one asked where he had been, of course, nor said a word when he decided to walk to the marketplace, something he never does, in search of a particular brand of coffee, which he never drank. All were surprised, but none questioned the will of the Master. I was chosen to accompany him, to carry whatever he purchased.

Ah! I remember how the exotic sights and smells of the market-place filled my senses that morning. The small mystery of the birds was all but forgotten as we walked past the shops and open stalls. Many of the merchants recognized the Master, offering fruit and loaves of bread in exchange for his prayers on their behalf. He had me write each of their names in the small notebook I always carried and then told them to distribute their offerings to the poor instead.

"So that my prayers may be truly heard by the Great Provider," he said.

After making his few purchases the Master decided to stroll around the Old City. We walked in silence for some time, coming at last upon the dome of the *Haram al-Sharif* mosque, said to be built on the ruins of Solomon's Temple.

There, in the shadow of the great dome, I first noticed the ancient beggar. He was burnt brown as the coffee, naked but for white cotton shorts, worn sandals and a white knit cap, sitting on the stone steps and telling the fortunes of those who gave alms into his bowl. He was tall and very thin, all rib and sinew and lean muscle. He might have just stepped out of some biblical desert, save that his white hair and beard were clean and neatly combed, perhaps out of respect for the worshippers.

The Master stopped and looked at him for a moment. I had never seen the man before, yet there was something strangely familiar about him. I felt a sudden sympathy for him, and a quick stirring of pity for the hard life still left to his old bones.

"I wonder if his prayers are ever answered?" I mused aloud.

"You may be certain that they are," the Master said, turning to me, his dark eyes shining below eyebrows white and thick as clouds. "But of course he asks nothing for himself, so they are very light prayers indeed, rising to the heavens like mist from this ocean of life. He is a *faqir*, one who has attained the detachment of *sakina*, that tranquility of heart that comes only with submission to the will of *Allah*. So it is he who should pity you, young Ishaq. When you have learned to look with your heart, your eyes will not deceive you. Go! Toss your coins into his bowl. The less you are burdened by possessions, the lighter will be the anchor of your self-indulgent *nafs*."

How wisely I nodded my head in agreement, and how little I understood. How little I understand even now, though I did indeed approach the old man to drop a few coins into his intricately carved *kashkul*, his beggar's gourd.

When he looked up I was so startled that the coins dropped from my hand. The old man's white hair and beard framed a leathery face scored with many deep wrinkles, cut by time and desert winds, at once grotesque and compelling. I wanted to look away, but his eyes caught mine and I could not move. They burned like coals within that ancient face, yet held so certain a serenity I felt suddenly ashamed of my small vanities.

He said: "You will go on a long journey!"

He lowered his eyes and did not speak again, and I could not, managing only to bow awkwardly and retreat behind my Master's robe like a child. I had barely heard the old man's words, yet I felt that this *faqir,* who had nothing but God, was the wealthy one, while I, dressed in finery and weighted with coins and pity, was the beggar.

My thoughts returned to the old man all that day. What deserts had etched that face, what hardships had bought such grim wisdom?

And those black wells of eyes, what visions had they seen? I was certain I had never seen the man before, yet the sense of familiarity would not leave me. It made me restless and uneasy. I resolved to ask the Master about my state after the evening meal.

"The memory that has been stirred by the *faqir*," he said, walking by my side in the garden, "is your soul's remembrance of its pure state before creation. His perfection of heart calls out to those on the path.

"And the unease," he continued, reading the uncertainty in my mind, "is your fear of him. You do not yet listen with the ear of acceptance, yet you have been led to the path of the heart, on which the gold of the world will not buy you even a grain of its dust. Your worldly self fears that the path will lead you into worldly poverty.

"O, Ishaq! The generous heart always has enough to give. It is the miserly in spirit who believe they never have enough to be generous. It is not lack of possessions that leads to spiritual poverty, nor prayer and fasting by themselves. It is in the abandonment of self-absorption, and in constant remembrance and reflection that the heart becomes detached. Then the hands gladly open their grasp on worldly things and cleave to God."

I did not say more, chastened by his words. He looked at me and sighed.

"Alas, like Moses, you are blind to the worth of true alms. Your thoughts are still so cluttered with yourself that there is no room for anything else to enter."

The Master then commanded that I sleep outside that night, to breathe the same air and feel the same earth as the *faqir*, and so aid the heart's memory.

Thus I brought my sleeping mat, blanket and pillow into the

garden and lay down on one of the Persian rugs spread near the central fountain. The Master holds many meetings here in the summer and the energy is very strong. I nestled under the blanket with my hands behind my head and absorbed the night, letting the softly flowing water soothe me.

The moon had risen full and golden over the eastern desert, and now shone high and silver bright amid the innumerable stars above Jerusalem. It filled my heart with an inexpressible longing. I felt as if all the lights of heaven were burning. It was so immense and beautiful that it stilled my thoughts. My eyes closed, and in that first instant between sleep and dream I remembered the old tale. Or rather, it remembered me.

Moses walked alone into the desert and prayed, beseeching God. "O Lord, for many years I have been Thy faithful servant, yet Thou hast never entered my house, nor broken bread with me. Wilt Thou not come and sup in my house?"

And God was well pleased with the request, and answered him: *"Yea, Verily! Truly thou hast been My faithful servant, and so I will come this very evening to thy dwelling and break bread with thee!"*

Moses was delighted that he was to be granted this special grace, and made swiftly for home, ordering his household as to the preparations, and cooking with his own hands a great feast worthy of the Lord.

When all was in readiness and the supper hour drew near, Moses dressed in his finest robes and waited outside his house, pacing in his eagerness. Many of the people were about at this hour, returning home from their day's labors, and they bowed in greeting as they passed him.

He returned their greetings distractedly until an old man in the crowd, a beggar, came up to him and bowed low. He was clothed in rags and leaned heavily upon a staff of sandalwood. "Great sir," said the old man, "will thee not share some small portion of thy bounty with one of lesser fortune? By the *adab*, the tradition of courtesy, I ask it."

"Yea, yea..." answered Moses kindly, but impatiently. "You shall have your fill, and coins for your purse also. But you must come back later. I await an important guest now, and have no time for thee."

So the beggar walked on and Moses waited. Hour after hour all through the night he paced and waited, but the Lord did not come. Now Moses was greatly disconcerted. He wept exceedingly and slept not at all. The very thought that God had forgotten him struck him to the heart. At dawn he again walked into the desert. Weeping, he rent his garments and prostrated himself upon the ground.

"O Lord!" he cried, "How have I offended Thee, that Thou did not come to my house as Thou had promised?"

"O Moses," said the Lord, *"I was the beggar who leaned upon his staff, whom thou bid depart. Know ye that **I** am in all My creation, and what thou apportion to the least of My servants, thou apportion to **Me**!"*

When I awoke to sunlight, tears stained my cheeks. I wept at the immensity of my ignorance, and at the long journey of the heart I had yet to make. Abu 'l-Qasim al- Junayd, who was said to be the *Qutb* of his time, once exclaimed: *"I will walk a thousand leagues in falsehood, that one step of the journey may be true."* Surely, that was what the *faqir* had read in me. I thanked God for having led me to a Master of the Path, and for the wondrous gift of my life.

All else are *nafs*, vanities of the fearful and Commanding self.

Master of the Jinn

I have made Thee the Companion of my heart,
But my body is here for those that desire its company,
And my body is friendly towards its guest,
But the Beloved of my heart is the guest of my soul.
—Rabi'a al-Adawiyya of Basra

We were happy. Indeed, we gave little thought to the world as we sat the next night in a semi-circle around our Master, who had ordered a feast be prepared and that every *darvish*, every disciple, be invited to the *khaniqah*, the house of the Order.

To us, the Master, for all his fierce looks and often inexplicable behavior, is as dear as our fathers, for as they raised us from childhood to the ways of the world, he guides our steps on the *tariqat*, the way of the heart, the straight path of the Sufi.

Know, O men, that my Master is *Shaykh* Amir al-Haadi, of the _____Sufi Order, and there are none that may compare with him in wisdom and attainment: For he is known to be the *Qutb* of the age, the magnetic pole of the inward journey.

That irresistible attraction, I am now certain, was the cause of the events that began that night.

A joy unlooked for is twice welcome, it is said, and so we celebrated, for the Master rarely orders such a gathering.

I may not name any save those necessary to the tale, so I will say only that there were twelve men and fourteen women present, all that could attend on such short notice. The Master had excluded the children from this particular night, although they are ordinarily welcome. That there were three unmarried men present seems, upon reflection, a fact the Master may have somehow predetermined. I have been in his company long enough to have seen him perform many marvels of exactitude, which seemed at the time to be random occurrences but later proved to be precisely what was necessary.

After the evening prayer, while dinner was still in preparation, we gathered in the great walled garden to sit cross-legged upon the grass and wait for him to speak.

The lemon trees were in bloom and the fragrance of the blossoms refreshed our hearts; and there were roses and hyacinths in abundance amid a variety of flowers and plants arrayed among the cypress and plane trees, all holding in subtle balance the energies within the walls. It was an oasis in the arid climate, an architecture designed to reflect the cosmic order, even as the fountain at its center sends its endless ripples expanding unto the Infinite Source.

We sat, as is our way, with the right hand resting upon the left thigh, the left hand holding the right wrist, forming the Arabic word *la*, meaning "no." This is the *no* of negation, by which the *darvish* strives to empty the hands of worldly possessions and the heart of what has left the hands—a first step on the Path.

Those chosen to serve that night brought out a silver tray holding small glasses of dark tea and a bowl of sugar cubes, which some held in their mouths while sipping the tea. We were eager for him to begin, but he seemed in no hurry as he leaned against the trunk of the old almond tree, which he himself had planted many years ago, stroking his beard thoughtfully and filling an ancient, ivory-bowled pipe. No *darvish* would break the silence by speaking first, of course. Above the entrance to the garden was a framed aphorism written in flowing calligraphy: *Silence, for breath is a Godsend.*

Finally, after a few long puffs, he signaled Ali for music. Ali immediately took up his *ney*, his reedpipe, and Rami the double-bowled *tar*, tuning the strings carefully. Others produced various sized *dafs*, the shallow, goatskin drums played by hand. The Master, however, commanded that all the other instruments be silent. I wondered briefly at this, for celebrations are almost always filled with lively music and clapping hands and voices raised in song, but I soon lost all curiosity as Ali began to play an unusually haunting refrain on that most human-throated of instruments, plaintive as the call of the *muezzin*.

The breath of the *ney* sighed with the wind amid the trees, exhaling the textured feel of the night and the soft glow of the lanterns, opening our hearts like the moonflowers and night-blooming jasmine opening around us, and we began to drift into *sama*, the timeless reverie.

The longing of many hearts slowly filled the garden, brimming at last over the walls and drifting upwards toward the stars as the reedpipe lamented its separation from the reedbed as surely the soul laments its separation from Paradise.

As the last notes melted into the night and we slowly awoke to the world in which we had each been cast adrift, unstoppable tears stained our cheeks and watered the grass beneath us. Even the flowers in their nurtured beds seemed to weep their dew. Slowly, slowly, the unity of our yearning washed away and we became our separate selves again, all looking to the Master who sat with head bowed beneath the limbs of the old tree.

His eyes were clear and dry as he raised his head and peered around the circle, absorbing each of us in his glance.

"May the heart remember what the mind has forgotten," he said. "And now listen, those that have ears, to a tale of Solomon the King. Yes, Solomon, the mightiest and wisest ruler of the earth that ever was or shall be. Wealthy beyond measure was Solomon, and with such wisdom as only *Allah* may bestow.

"And lo, he commanded the wind, and both men and *Jinn*, birds and animals. All were servants unto him. Yet he lost favor in the sight of God, for neither wealth nor power nor wisdom brought him enlightenment.

"One day, while King Solomon was walking alone in the royal garden, he came upon *Azrael*, the Angel of Death, who was pacing back and forth with a most worried expression. Solomon knew well the face of the Deadly Servant, for with the sight given unto him he had seen Death often, hovering over battles, or in the tents of the ill and wounded. When Solomon asked what troubled him, the Angel sighed, saying that he had on his list of those destined for the next world two scribes of Solomon, the brothers Elihoreph and Alijah.

"Now Solomon was grieved at the thought of losing his scribes, for he had known them since childhood and loved them as brothers. So he ordered the *Jinn* to carry Elihoreph and Aljah to the fabled city of *Luz*, the only place on earth where Death has no power. Instantly the *Jinn* did as he commanded, but the two scribes died at the very moment they reached the gates of that city.

"The next day *Azrael* appeared before Solomon. The Angel of Death was greatly pleased and said, *'I thank thee, O King, for speeding thy servants to the place appointed. The fate destined for them was to die at the gates of that far city, but I had no idea how they were to traverse so great a distance.'*

27

"Now the King wept exceedingly, torn between sorrow and wrath at the death of his friends and the inescapable doom of men. And *Azrael* wondered greatly at this.

'Why do you weep, O Lord of the World?''

'For the long friends of my youth who are with me no more,' said the King. 'Have you no pity for those whose life you end?'

'Pity?' exclaimed *Azrael* scornfully. *'You weep for the loss of their companionship. Your true sorrow is for yourself, and your wrath is truly self-pity. Alas, it has darkened your wisdom. Death is the most sublime gift of God, distilling from this life of fleeting joys and many sorrows that single drop which is the soul. Of such wine, O King, is poured the Sea of Light. Praise Allah that I, who am to you the Angel of Death, am in truth the Angel of Mercy.'"*

The Master looked at each of us in turn, and then shook his head and smiled. A few others also smiled, but I did not, nor did the older *darvishes*. *King Solomon?* The Master had never before related this old story, at least not in any group I have been in, although he instructs us constantly in many and various ways, each according to what is necessary at that moment for their development. And this tale had always seemed quite charming and straightforward on its surface. I did not know what juice there was left to squeeze, though all such tales are said to have seven levels of meaning.

We waited for the Master to speak further, thinking he would illuminate his intent, but he said, "When *Allah* first commanded the spirit of life to enter the Body of Adam, it was afraid and did not wish to go. 'I fear this strange existence apart from you, Lord," it said. And God replied, *'Reluctantly shall you enter and reluctantly shall you depart.'* And so it is. Death is inevitable, yet you fear it still. Your worldly selves tremble at the thought. But a Sufi asks for nothing and fears nothing, for he entrusts his life to God and gives all he has in humility.

"So, my brave and humble *darvishes*, should Solomon knock on the door this very night and bid you journey to a far country, who amongst you would step forth, even into danger and death, if that is your fate?"

For a moment, silence and blank faces were all that could be heard or seen as we looked at each other in bewilderment.

"Well, has no one an answer?" he asked, looking around the circle. "Has no one among you ears to hear?"

What was this? I wondered. *Some riddle game he played, or a test of our progress to be made known by the answer?*

"I would go!" exclaimed Ali, with a laugh. He must have believed the former.

"And I, also!" said Rami, his cousin. His sober expression showing that he thought the latter.

Many voices were raised then, declaring their willingness to go on such a journey with Solomon. But I held my tongue in the prison of its teeth, as it is said. Something about the Master's continence kept me silent. Rarely does he ask a simple question, and few seemed to take his tale seriously. I set my mind to wait, but to my astonishment heard myself asking: "Who on the Path is not already on such a journey?" Truly, I had not thought to speak, and certainly not in such a challenging tone.

There was not a sound in the room.

All eyes turned to me. I felt those sitting on my right and left move imperceptibly away, as from the coming of the lightning. The Master turned his face toward me as I sat frozen to the spot.

His eyes locked with mine for what seemed a full turning of the earth, then he raised his head and laughed. I realized that I had not dared to breathe in the grip of those eyes, and exhaled with a mighty "Whew!"

Everyone roared with laughter. The consternation I felt put me to the blush, and the women pointed and held their sides.

The Master raised his hand for silence and looked at me once more.

"Who indeed? . . . But do not be disconcerted, O Ishaq, at the laughter of your fellow travelers. Laughter is a gift, and so you have done them a service . . . And," he said, smiling gently," I perceive that it is the *ruh*, the innermost spirit within you that has spoken, moving for once past your more cautious mind. And rightly so! All here *are* on such a journey, though where the path will lead, each of you must discover alone.

"So fear not. If you have in the beginning been ordained to a noble destiny, you will attain it only with courage, and the *baraka*, the measure of grace you have each been given. What must be done, will be done. . ." He paused, looking first to Ali and then to Rami. "You, Ali, the first to speak, and you Rami, the second, and Ishaq too must go. . . Many threads are woven into this tapestry." He sighed, lowering his head and closing his eyes.

Immediately, there was a loud knock at the door.

Ali and Rami looked startled, and I felt the small hairs of my neck stand up. We heard no bell from the courtyard gate. Someone must have left it open. One of the women, Mojdeh, went to answer. I strained to hear the conversation through the house, but could not. The Master did not seem to have heard the knock, or paid no attention to it, but he looked up as Mojdeh returned to the garden with an odd expression on her face. Bowing formally, with her hand over her heart, she said, "Master, Solomon is here."

Master of the Jinn

The touchstone discerns what is gold.
—The *Gulistan* (The Rose Garden)
of Musharrif al-Din Sa'di

So came into our circle three strangers with whom my life was to be woven.

Without shoes they entered, as is our custom, and the Master rose and stepped forward to greet them, gesturing for the rest of us to stay seated. Certainly he must have expected them, and yet I was struck by the perfection of timing that caused such a shock among us, not believing for a moment in its coincidence. A thrill of fear gripped my spine.

He greeted the older man as one would an old friend, embracing him and kissing both his cheeks. *"Mehman Habibeh Khodast,"* he said, "A guest is God's friend." It was an old Persian saying. He then turned to the young woman and bowed formally, his right hand over his heart, and lastly shook the younger man's hand, looking silently and intently at him.

The women seated around me stared openly, their mouths gaping. Even the Master's daughters could not stop looking at the deeply tanned face of the handsome young stranger. His red hair had been turned nearly bronze by the sun, and he had brown eyes set deep into the angular planes of cheek and jawline. Another Joseph for some fortunate Zulaikha, as the old tale goes. Apparently, the women agreed. *A heart stopper,* one of them whispered to another.

The Master, however, seemed oblivious to the reaction of the women and turned to introduce the new arrivals. The *darvishes*

stood immediately, perhaps a bit suspicious at the seemingly con-
trived drama of their arrival, but acting at once with all courtesy, as
the *adab*, the etiquette of the Path, required. Chivalry began as a
Sufi virtue, it is said.

Chairs were ordered, but each of our guests chose to sit upon the
grass with us. Mas'ud, the tea master, brought three glasses of the
dark tea. Both men took a glass, but the young woman declined.
The Master ordered her served the coffee bought that morning,
much to her surprise, and more tea was brought for the others and
sweets for all.

The older man was Professor Shlomeh Freeman, *Solomon*,
Director of the Department of Antiquities at Jerusalem University,
and apparently a student of our Master's at Oxford many years ago.
He was a large, clean-shaven man with closely cropped hair, over six
feet tall and somewhat portly from the sedentary life of a scholar.

The young woman was Rebecca, his daughter, perhaps twenty-
five years of age. She had a tall dancer's body and sat gracefully,
her back perfectly straight, the dark curly hair that was her mother's gift cut short. With her sharp features and large brown eyes,
she might have been called beautiful, but the hard line of her mouth
warned of an intractable nature.

Ah, and the heart stopper, who introduced himself quietly as
Aaron Simach, a friend and colleague of the Professor, could not
disguise even from my untutored eye, the look and bearing of
a soldier.

Laila, one of the older *darvishes*, then entered carrying an ewer
and basin, a white towel draped over one arm. I remember her
warm, dark eyes as she bowed before the Master and proceeded to
pour water into the basin so that he could wash his hands. She then

repeated her bow and helped our three guests to also wash their hands. The Professor bowed formally in gratitude, his hand over his heart. And the young man and woman, who until then had been stiff and unsmiling, also appeared to relax somewhat at this gentle courtesy.

The sweets were then passed, and we all sat silent and amazed while Professor Solomon Freeman and *Shaykh* Amir al-Haadi exchanged stories about their university days long ago.

No, I cannot tell of their younger years. Of this one matter I truly have little memory except for a vague impression of laughter from them and amazement from the rest of us, who knew little of our Master's youth. Even as my pen strokes ink to paper, the bits of recollection fall away like leaves into a river, swept off as if by some swift current of telepathic waters.

It is said that the Master's secrets keep themselves. I do not doubt it.

After the tea has been drunk and the glasses collected, another of the Master's daughters appeared in the doorway and caught his eye. "Dinner is ready," she said.

"Bismillah!" he replied, "In the name of God," and all the *darvishes* jumped to their feet and stood waiting for the Master's direction. Our guests responded, to their credit, by also rising and waiting. Then he stood and led them into the main room of the *khaniqah* as we followed.

Over the Persian carpets that covered the floor, a long white *sufreh* had been set with plates and spoons and glasses already filled with water. Those chosen to serve that night were setting

34

down the dishes of the feast, many of which came from the garden we had just left; oranges and grapes, apricots and lemon slices, almonds, chick-peas and bread out of the oven. Also bowls of green parsley and cucumbers in yogurt, cold kabob, steaming lamb pilaf, and chicken in pomegranate sauce. A special sweet waited in the kitchen for dessert. We divide foods into *sardi,* cold, and *garmi,* hot, depending on the cooling or warming effects they have on the body. This distinction is an expression of their inherent attributes, not their temperature. Since it was early summer and very warm, *sardi* dishes were served.

The Master, as is our custom, was the first to be seated, and as always on formal occasions he sat on the white sheepskin rug of his station and rank; at his back a large, ornate pillow embroidered by his late wife with one of the ninety-nine names of God. Above him was set a plain *kashkul* and crossed axes, symbols of the order, with which the *darvish* chops away desire for this world with one, and hope of the next world with the other, so that only God remains. This is the heart of the Path.

The Master motioned for Professor Freeman to sit on his right and Mr. Simach on his left. He asked Rebecca to sit across from him. "Food for the body, beauty for the soul," he said. Rebecca, caught off guard by his graciousness, smiled self-consciously and blushed. His daughters giggled.

When they were seated he turned his attention to the rest of us, who stood at place, waiting. Most he left where they were, a few he rearranged, then motioned for all to sit. I was placed on the right of Rebecca, Ali on her left, and Rami next to Ali.

The Master does nothing without purpose, and many times will position us in ways meant to produce or balance certain energies;

young and old, male and female, or by levels of advancement. What his intention was in this arrangement I cannot say, although I believe the two cousins enjoyed being placed close to her, as did I. Perhaps it was that we three were the only unmarried men there, but she did exude a certain guarded sensuality from within the severity of her look and manner. I felt it even though she had not spoken ten words all evening.

The various dishes were passed first to the Master, who filled the plates of his guests before his own, then passed them around the *sufreh* until all were filled. No one had yet begun to eat. The new-comers must have been instructed in the *adab*, for they also sat with folded hands and bowed heads.

When all were served, the Master poured a bit of salt into his hand, tasted it, and said, *"Bismillah,"* then dipped a piece of flat bread into a bowl of yogurt to begin the meal. We say no formal grace, but consider food that is eaten without remembrance to be shared with the devil.

It is also our custom that the Master begin and end each meal, but he eats little and so eats slowly that everyone may have their fill. I noticed Rebecca glancing at him, and she also ate sparingly. Out of the corner of my eye, I watched her strong hands hold bread and spoon.

Soon all were finished except Professor Freeman. We usually eat in silence, but the Master had asked him a question at the beginning of the meal, pitching his voice so that no other could hear, and the answer, also unheard, was of such length that he had neglected the plate before him. The Master now nibbled a bit of bread until the Professor finished and put his spoon aside.

The Master then looked around, making certain all were truly finished, and touched the fingers of his right hand to the *sufreh* and then to his lips.

"Alhamdulillah," he said. "All praise is God's alone."

The meal was over. We all stood at once, the Master rising and leading his guests and the *darvishes* out of the room and once more into the garden. Professor Freeman and Mr. Simach walked out speaking quietly to each other, but Rebecca stood in the doorway for a moment, watching those selected to clean as they bent quickly to the task.

First, the long white tablecloth was wiped and folded, foot by foot, then halved again until only a small square remained. One of the servers then prostrated himself before the Master's white rug until his forehead touched the folded square. He then kissed the *sufreh* as a sign of respect and submission, and finally stood and walked backwards through the doorway. Also out of respect, our backs are never turned to the Master or his symbolic seat.

Rebecca said nothing. She seemed quite taken by the ritual. I remembered finding it equally as charming the first time I witnessed it, but it would not be courteous to keep the Master or his guests waiting. I gently touched her arm and led her into the garden.

When all were seated, tea was served, and the special sweet, flaky and filled with almonds. The moon was lower in the sky, but could still be seen over the wall of the garden.

"We were speaking of King Solomon before you arrived," the Master said to Professor Freeman. "Perhaps you would be kind enough to add some flavor to the stew?"

The Professor glanced quickly at his daughter and Mr. Simach. "Yes, well, I do give the occasional lecture," he said, laughing modestly and clearing his throat.

"His true name," he began, glancing at the moon just visible over the garden wall, "was *Jedidiah*, the 'friend of God,' but was later made *Shelomo*, Solomon, the 'King of Peace,' because of the peace that prevailed during the greater part of his reign. And other names he had also: *Ben*, because he was the builder of the Temple; *Jekeh* because he was the ruler of the known world; and *Ithiel*, because God was with him."

He stopped and looked at the Master, who nodded slightly.

"What is truly known," he went on, now focusing his gaze to include us all, "is, unfortunately, very little. Legends abound, in the Bible, the Talmud, the History of Josephus and the Koran. Facts are few, and even those are open to much speculation. And yet, as *Shaykh* Haadi so often pointed out when I was his student, facts are distinguishable by their coldness, truth by its warmth. There are many tales of Solomon, and almost all are used to illustrate a moral. One story in particular, however, may warm you . . ."

He paused again, smiling, looking at our faces as a teacher would in gauging the effect of his words on his students.

"Consider what is called the Seal of Solomon," he said. "The six-pointed star."

He asked if there was anything to write on, and a small blackboard and chalk were brought to him. He drew the star.

"Here is a symbol ancient and filled with meaning. It contains the six powers of motion; above, below, front, back, right, left. It contains the six directions; up, down, front, back, left, and right. It is said to be the perfect number because the days of creation were six. It contains the first even number, 2, and the first odd number, 3. And the interlocking triangles represent not only the masculine and feminine duality of nature, but also the active intellect and the passive soul manifested from the one God. The product of their union is creation, and the harmony of the universe.

"And this hexagon and its various complementary aspects also include the four ancient elements of nature," he said, and drew four triangles.

"The triangle pointing upward is fire, down is water. The triangle pointing up with the line of the other in it symbolizes air, while the downward triangle with the other's line is earth. Together they form the Seal of Solomon: The synthesis of all the elements, the tendencies of all forms, where all opposites come into union."

He paused to catch his breath, and then looked at the Master. Both broke out in laughter.

The Master was still chuckling as Professor Freeman looked at his daughter. "It was *Shaykh* Haadi's first lecture in Religious Symbolism. A wonderful class," he said.

"High praise, indeed," the Master acknowledged with a slight bow, "coming from my worst student."

They laughed again, and we along with them. After a moment, the Professor continued.

"Now, some sources contend that this Seal of Solomon, is, in fact, *not* his seal." He paused to look at his daughter. The Master watched him intently, and I wondered if anyone else had heard that he said, in *fact*, not in *truth*.

"They say that this six-pointed star is the *Megen* David, the Shield of David, and that the Seal of Solomon is another star, the pentacle, or pentagram." He paused again, searching our faces for some sign he apparently did not find.

"Continue, Shlomeh," the Master said, "Let us hear the full tale."

It was the first time the Master had used his friend's given name, and somehow the saying of the word had an effect on the man. He sat upright from his slouched position, squaring his shoulders and stretching his back muscles.

"Yes," he said. "The seal . . . It is written that at the time Solomon began the building of the Temple, Assaf, the *Vizir* of Solomon, complained that someone was stealing precious jewels from his rooms, and from other courtiers as well. Even the royal treasury was not immune. Now Assaf was also renowned for his wisdom and knew that no ordinary thief could have done these deeds. 'Some evil spirit causes this mischief,' he counseled the King.

"Solomon then prayed fervently to God to deliver the wicked spirit into his hands for punishment. At once his prayer was answered. The archangel Michael appeared before the King, and put into his hand the mightiest power that ever was or shall be in this world . . . a small, golden ring, inset with a seal of engraved stone.

"And Michael said: *'Take this ring, O Solomon King, son of David, the gift which the Lord God hath sent unto thee. Wear this ring, and all the demons of the earth, both male and female, thou wilt command.'*

"Now, many medieval sources claim that the *pentalpha*, or pentacle, the ancient sign of sorcery, was engraved on the ring, because Solomon was said to have been a master of the magic arts. But I do not think this was so. The pentacle is older than Solomon, first seen on pottery from *Ur of the Chaldees*, in ancient Babylon.

"Other sources describe the ring as made of pure gold, set with a single *shamir* stone; a diamond perhaps, or the same heavenly

40

green *shamir* stone said to have been part of the Temple. The stone was cut and set in the form of an eight-rayed star. On it was engraved the hexagon seal, and within that the four letters of the ineffable name of God, *YHWH*."

He stopped for a moment and brushed a hand across his hair.

"No stone," he began again, now looking directly at Mr. Simach, "was ever so renowned as the stone in the ring of Solomon. For with it the whole earth came under his sway. Only death was beyond his power to control . . ."

The Professor glanced at his daughter, then at the Master, as if waiting for some sign. He appeared excited.

"Yes, my *darvishes*," the Master broke in, "death is beyond all power, save the One. There is no remedy for death other than to look it constantly in the face. We who are born will die; we must submit. Even he who held the world under the seal of his ring is now only a mineral in the earth . . . But please continue . . ."

Professor Freeman bowed slightly from his sitting position. "Armed with the ring, Solomon commanded the guilty spirit to appear. He wore the ring on the mid-finger of the right hand, and pointed it at the foot of his high throne, saying, 'By the power of the seal of the one God, I command thee, troublesome spirit, to come forth.'

"A roaring column of flame instantly appeared, reaching nearly to the high ceiling of the throne room many cubits above, and just as quickly was gone. Whether the flame itself took shape, or merely preceded him, could not be seen, but where the flame had been, the demon stood, caught in his mischief; for he still clutched in his hands a great many jewels just stolen from the royal vaults. So great was his surprise that he dropped the gems, which scattered like pebbles on the marble floor, and his red eyes darted back and forth like twin flames in that broad, swarthy face. And wide wonder came into those terrible eyes that some power existed among mortal men that was greater than his will.

"Twice the height of the King he was and more, greater even than Goliath that David slew, the King's father. And of so dark and menacing a countenance was the demon that even Assaf the wise drew back in horror. Only Solomon stood firm, and a light shone before him.

"Then the demon saw the face of the King, whose arm pointed toward him, and beheld the seal of the ring. The demon's cruel, lidless eyes went wide, and he let out such a ghastly, howling shriek that the very stones of the palace trembled to their foundation. It was so horrible a sound that all the people of the kingdom who heard it covered their ears and cast themselves on the ground in fear. Oxen died of terror in the fields and birds fell from the sky, for it was like unto the cry of a soul newly plunged in the flames of hell.

"But the power of God was within the ring, so that even the demon was helpless. He fell to his knees and prostrated himself before the King.

"*'Mercy, Master!'* cried the *Jinni.*

"'Name thyself, demon.' commanded Solomon.

"*'I am called Ornias, O Great King!'*

"'Why hast thou done such mischief to my household? Speak truly!'

"*'Hunger, Lord of the World! Hunger insatiable!'* And he revealed himself as a vampire spirit, who with fangs harder than adamant pierces the gems of the earth to drink their light.

"'Why dost thou drink the light of earthly jewels?' demanded

Assaf the *Vizir*, 'It is a thing unheard of among the wise.'"

But the *Jinni* was silent.

"'Speak the answer,' said the King, 'I command it.'

"'*Thou knowest my answer, King of Wisdom,*' said the demon.

"Then Solomon looked into his heart, for the forty-nine gates of wisdom were open to him, as they had been to Moses. This derives from the belief that each word of the Torah has forty-nine meanings. And he discerned there the answer, and it amazed him, so that he looked on the creature before him with a new understanding and pity."

The Professor paused, breathing deeply. "But perhaps your Master will give you the answer," he said, looking at our rapt faces. "As he did to me, years ago."

We all looked to the Master. There was a glint in his eye and he nodded approvingly.

"Know then the sorrow of the demon," he said. "For the gems of the earth were born at the dawn of the world, created by the death of ancient forests buried beneath the weight of mountains. It was a time of upheaval when both *Jinn* and Angels were cast out and world was broken. The light of the new sun was still in the green life of those forests as slowly they were transformed, crystallized by the long years into the light that sparkles from the cut and polished jewels. And so *Ornias* the demon, denied the light of heaven, drinks the light of the first morning, feeding his sorrow and his loss."

The Master stopped, relighting and drawing on his pipe.

Wonderful! Indeed, every *darvish* was touched by the tale, *warmed,* if you will. Even Mr. Simach seemed moved, and Rebecca's eyes were wide beside me. *When the Master speaks, the angels listen,* we say, for he speaks with the tongue of sincerity.

"And so," Professor Freeman went on, "Solomon burned the seal into the neck of *Ornias* as a brand of his sovereignty, and the *Jinni* from that moment did his bidding, and was given the task of cutting stones for the building of the Temple.

"And other of the Jinn who were causing mischief within the realm were also commanded to come forth: *Onoskelis*, who had the shape and skin of a fair-hued woman; *Asmodeus,* who professed the Hebrew faith and was said to observe the Torah; *Tephros*, the demon of the Ashes, and after him a group of seven females spirits who declared themselves to be the thirty-six elements of the darkness; and *Rabdos*, a ravenous, hound-like spirit. All were branded with the seal of the ring.

"Others there were also for another tale, but one more for this: A demon having all the limbs of a man, but without a head.

"The demon said, *'I am called Envy, for I delight in devouring heads. But I hunger always, and desire* **YOUR HEAD NOW**.*'*"

The Professor shouted the last words for emphasis and made such a face that we were all startled into laughter.

The Master smiled. "Indeed, envy is the prison of the spirit," he said.

And Rebecca, who had been looking at her father strangely during the tale, spoke now with wonder and recognition in her eyes. "I remember now. He used to tell me this tale as a bedtime story, and I thought every word was true."

Though it would be rude for a *darvish* to speak without permission, it is not so for a guest, and we all laughed.

When the glasses were again refilled with tea and Rebecca's cup with coffee, a silence fell over the garden. Throats were cleared, positions were shifted for greater comfort, and the Master raised both hands for attention. The night was passing and the sun would soon rise.

"Now is the time for those that must go to leave," he said. "And those that remain to come into the *khaniqah*."

Many rose and bid farewell to the Master and his guests. The rest of us returned to the large, open living room and sat on the Persian rugs, our backs resting on ornate pillows against the wall, facing the Master on his sheepskin.

He then sent the rest of the household off to bed, with the exception of Ali, Rami, and myself. Why we three were asked to remain was not questioned, for it was by now apparent even to me, who had taken but the first half-step on the Path, that our guests had come with some hidden purpose.

"Know that I bind you now under your vow of silence as to what you will see and hear," the Master said to us in a solemn voice. "Now Shlomeh, my old friend, tell us what need has brought you here."

We turned to the Professor, who was at that instant listening to his young companion's urgent whisper. Dismissing the words with a shake of his head, he looked at his daughter, who nodded, not changing her unreadable expression.

From the large shoulder bag she carried, she removed an object wrapped in a white towel, placing it in front of the Master. I looked at the expectant faces of the three guests and was unable to suppress a shiver as the Master delicately removed the layers of towel. What was revealed made us gasp.

A golden cylinder, encrusted with jewels, caught the first rays of morning light through the window and blazed among us like a star.

"Allah!" exclaimed Ali and Rami together. I held my breath. No one spoke until a passing cloud caused the light to fade.

The Master said nothing. Turning the cylinder with the tip of a finger, he exposed a Star of David, a Seal of Solomon, made entirely of diamonds, cunningly set within an ivory circle. Still no one uttered a word.

"Where did you get this, Captain Simach?" he said, looking directly into the young man's eyes.

Captain? I looked at Ali and Rami looking at me.

"I found it in a cave uncovered by a sandstorm, in the hand of a skeleton," he said without hesitation, his voice barely containing the emotion in the words.

The Master did not change expression when he looked at Professor Freeman. "Shlomeh, we must hear the full tale."

The Professor looked at Captain Simach, who looked down and would not meet his eyes, and then at his daughter, who simply said, "Go on."

So it was told, and here I set the tale. And may *Allah* guide the telling, for His pen is cut from the reedbed of the heart, and therein lays the Truth.

The Master

From the end of the earth will I cry unto Thee,
when my heart is overwhelmed: lead
me to the rock that is higher than I.
—Psalms 61:2

Professor Solomon Freeman had first met *Mossad* Captain Aaron Simach two years ago, when the young man was still a police detective. The Professor was called upon as an expert to help build a case against a group of extremely clever forgers.

They had been bilking rich tourists with incredible replicas of biblical works; parchments cured and treated in the ancient way and claimed to contain everything from newly discovered Dead Sea scrolls to lost books of the Old Testament. The greedy tourists deserved to be cheated, of course, and he could not help but feel a secret, professional admiration at the audacity of the forgers. He found it incredible that anyone could be *schmuck* enough to buy a supposedly "just discovered" Book of Moses.

The forgers had been excellent craftsman, but poor scholars. Their knowledge of Aramaic was limited in both an understanding of ancient grammar and knowledge of the older languages that formed its root words. The results were often laughable and always detectable, at least to him.

Captain Simach had been in charge of the investigation, and together they had taught the forgers the error of sloppy scholarship. Over the weeks of the trial, Solomon had come to like the earnest and intelligent young man. He had even considered introducing him to Rebecca. That he did not was due only to her forbidding him any involvement in her private life.

Now he arrived without notice at the end of the day. Solomon was alone in his office, having just written the last question of the graduate exam. Rebecca had called only a moment earlier, while he was still chuckling over the subtle difficulty of the question, to be certain that he would be home on time for dinner. Then the door opened.

He was simply there, standing tall and military straight, dressed in an open white shirt and tan slacks. Solomon was quite surprised and delighted to see him, shaking his hand warmly and offering him a chair and a drink of his only secret pleasure, imported Russian vodka.

The Captain accepted only the chair and Solomon noticed that something was wrong. That quick awareness Solomon had once so admired was gone, replaced by a peculiar, faraway look, the head cocked as if he were listening to something. And he looked much older.

After some small talk of a recent rash of forgeries coming to light, which Solomon thought may have prompted the unannounced visit, Captain Simach said, his voice sounding strained and tired, "I am also glad to see you again, Professor, but no forgery brought me."

From a small traveling bag he removed a golden cylinder and placed it on the desk between them. "This did."

"Ahhh!" Solomon exhaled the sound. Slowly, without taking his eyes off the object, he pulled on surgical gloves taken from a desk drawer, and with a small felt-tipped instrument turned the artifact. The Star of David, formed entirely of diamonds within its ivory setting, made him gasp. With a large magnifying glass he examined it carefully, not trusting even his own trained eye. The first giddiness of treasure was passing and the professional mind began to evaluate the artifact before him. Its age must be determined by dating the ivory, the artifact tested for purity of gold and quality of stones before it is opened. Such document cases were the property of ancient royalty, usually holding a single papyrus or parchment, or perhaps a scroll of copper or silver. Solomon noted with satisfaction that the seal was worn but unbroken. And he must examine the *bulla*, the seal impression. Still, the good Captain had acted prudently. Whatever was inside might be intact and legible. Acids appeared for testing the gold, and a jeweler's glass.

Captain Simach cleared his throat. "Please, I must ask that you tell no one of this."

Solomon looked up and nearly burst out laughing. "What? Have you become a looter?"

The young man shrugged.

What was going on here? Solomon wondered. Though he had never seen anything quite like the treasure before him, document cases such as this usually contained family birth records, census reports, merchant inventories and the like.

"What you've brought may be priceless, my friend, to be sure, but I doubt if it contains the Ten Commandments. It most likely belonged to a courtier, or some royal scribe or bookkeeper. If it contains anything at all, it's probably a grocery list."

Captain Simach said nothing.

"Why is the *Mossad* bringing this to me anyway? Do they think it's a clever fake?"

The young man shifted uneasily. "It's not a fake, Professor, and the *Mossad* has not brought it to you. I have."

Careful now! "I see. And how did you come by it, if I may ask?"

Captain Simach stared at him.

"Well?"

"I cannot tell you."

"Why?" the Professor asked, undeterred.

The Captain stammered for a second, then shrugged. "Where I found it is where I have been, and that is classified."

Ah! He found it in the desert! Solomon felt his heart beat faster. "This is difficult to understand, Aaron. I greatly appreciate your bringing this artifact to me, but you certainly must know that it was illegal to do so."

The Captain smiled faintly at the implication. After a long silence he shook his head and looked directly at Solomon. He appeared to have come to some decision, motioning toward the artifact between them.

"I found this in the hands of a skeleton after a sandstorm, in a cave."

"A sandstorm? In the Negev?"

"It was not in the Negev."

"Then where . . . ?"

But the Captain had said too much. His features softened.

"Please, Solomon . . ." he hesitated, looking rather puzzled all of a sudden, and then very serious and sad. "I came to you the first moment I was free to do so. I can't explain it. It's almost like something . . . I think it was . . . Well . . ."

He leaned closer across the desk, eyes shining, and then slumped back into his chair, out of words. Solomon poured them both a large measure of vodka and ice from the small refrigerator in the corner. He was silent, touched by the plight of the young man. What had he endured to cause this? Perhaps he had become slightly unbalanced when the sandstorm uncovered the skeleton. Legalities set aside, he handed him the drink and sipped his own.

"Very well, Aaron," he said gently, "I'm going to open this and see what's inside. I have the equipment in the laboratory next door. Will you come and help me? Perhaps we can solve this mystery and put your mind at ease."

Captain Simach smiled gratefully, but shook his head. "I must report back immediately." He handed him a card. "This number will always reach me. Please, if you need anything . . ."

He stood. Solomon shook his hand firmly.

"I'll call you tonight. There may be something. You never know."

As the Captain was about to close the door behind him, Solomon added, "And the skeleton? There may be more we can learn from it."

The Captain did not turn around. "Yes," he whispered. "I know where it is."

> *Behold! I will pour out to you*
> *my spirit*
> *I will make known unto you*
> *my words.*
> —Proverbs 1:23

He opened the cylinder without difficulty, and carefully unrolled the small rectangle of papyrus contained within. The cylinder itself was of pure gold, the diamonds flawless, the ivory yellowed and worn with age, but showing surprisingly little decay. *The desert cave again!* The seal, unfortunately, had revealed nothing. The *bulla* rubbing was blank, showing only that a flat, plain object was used, perhaps a smooth stone.

To his amazement, however, the papyrus was written in Canaanitish, not Aramaic. *Canaanitish!* Although similar to Phoenician and Moabitic, it was the most archaic known form of the Hebrew alphabet. He calmed himself slowly, knowing that there were centuries of overlap between the use of Aramaic letters and the more ancient Canaanitish. There had been Aramaic writing on papyrus as late as the Fourth Century B.C., found in the Egyptian upper Nile, a letter to the High Priest of the Temple in Jerusalem. And Canaanitish had been in use among Jews until about the First Century B.C. The Samaritans had even used one version in their Holy Scriptures.

But Solomon knew it was not that recent. Even eighth-century Hebrew inscriptions exhibit many specific and exclusive traits, but this script resembled that of the tenth century Phoenician inscriptions from Byblos. He immediately sealed it in an airtight glass envelope. Even limited exposure to air could cause it to deteriorate. Then aided by a powerful magnifying glass, his expert's eye discerned the wide scribal circles. *Almost as if . . . My God! It's the same as the Gezer Calendar.*

The Gezer Calendar, considered to be the earliest known Hebrew inscription, is paleographically dated to the late tenth century, when Gezer was an Israelite city. He knew the biblical reference by heart: 1 Kings 9:16. It was his favorite period of study, the time of King Solomon. The tightly sealed case and the cover of dry desert sand had preserved it in near perfect condition, just waiting for Captain Simach to stumble on it. He shook his head in disbelief.

It could have been written yesterday! He must try to get more details about its discovery. Although he berated himself for it, he could not escape a feeling of almost boyish excitement.

But what was this strange device on the reverse side? The two concentric circles and the Star of David within them resembled a seal, but not like any in his experience, and the cryptic words within and underneath the star puzzled him. He knew of no other papyrus inscribed on both sides. He shrugged. He did not doubt his ability. Soon he would know.

Captain Simach had left two hours ago. It was seven in the evening and he was alone, immersed in the puzzle. All he knew so far was that it was old, very old, and had been found somewhere in some desert. He had called the meteorological service, but there had been no report of a recent sandstorm.

And it was papyrus, yet he knew climatic conditions in Israel would decay even a sealed urn over time, even in the Negev. Too much moisture. No, it came from some deep desert. And Aaron had said it was not from the Negev. He now accepted at least that part of Captain Simach's story. There is some evidence that the Hebrews may have used papyrus even in the most ancient times; the plant itself, *gomeh*, is mentioned in both Exodus and Isaiah, even though the paper-like finished product is not. Solomon laughed at the idea that he may have here the most ancient, complete written papyrus ever discovered. The palimpsest found in the dry cave at *Wadi Murabba'at*, near the Dead Sea, is estimated to be only from the mid-Seventh Century B.C.

Solomon had taken a minute sample of the ink for testing. The results filled him with even greater excitement. It was gum of balsam mixed with soot and water; an ink of ancient days. Written, no doubt, by a hollow, hard reed pen called a *golmos* in Talmudic times. By the formation of the letters viewed under the magnifying glass, Solomon observed that the reed was cut so that the nib was broad, but not split.

The translation of the manuscript was next. The first line was easy enough, a common invocation, even today, but the next two words left him speechless.

I, Zadok

He stared at the words, torn between elation and disbelief. Zadok had been the High Priest of the Temple during the early reign of King Solomon, when the temple was built. He was said to be a second Aaron, the brother of Moses who was the first High Priest, a man eminently worthy to stand before the Ark of the Covenant.

He forced himself to take a short break to clear his mind before beginning the rest of the exacting translation. After munching on an apple left over from lunch, he lit a cigarette and stood at the open window, watching the rising moon. As always, the simple beauty of the clear night sky calmed his thoughts. Tonight the effect was nearly hypnotic. He blinked, and crossed abruptly and unbidden into reverie.

Solomon did not know how long he had been standing at the window. The wall clock told him that an hour had passed. He was astonished. His mind had never wandered like that before, and he could not quite remember what he had been thinking, although he felt the weight of it just over the edge of his awareness. Or was it a dream? *What happened to me? Did I fall asleep standing up?*

He did not feel tired. In fact, he felt as completely awake as he had ever been in his life. He sat down at his desk to begin the task of transcription, remembering then that he had not called his daughter to tell her he would be late for dinner. He would have to call and tell her he would be very late. Now he was really in trouble.

Master of the Jinn

> *Many waters cannot quench love,*
> *neither can floods drown it.*
> —Song of Solomon 8:7

Rebecca was silent when her father came home. It was eleven o'clock in the evening and she set warmed food on the table for him, taking for granted that he had gotten involved with some shard of pottery or tattered manuscript and had not eaten.

He wasn't fooled. Her anger was hard as ice; soon it would heat and wash over him. He told her nothing of what had occurred. Better for him if she did not know. Rebecca was still in the Army reserves after all, just home from active duty. He was not in the least surprised that she returned as a sergeant.

While he ate she sat with him, and speaking in a voice of controlled anger, like an exasperated parent to a constantly misbehaving child, explained once again the courtesy of a phone call if he was going to be late, and the ill effects of repeatedly missing supper and overworking himself. He nodded at her between mouthfuls, silent until she was out of breath and he could break in to compliment her on the excellent care she took of her only parent.

It did not appease her, though he meant it sincerely. She had no one else, and he could sense the underlying fear in her at the thought of losing him. She remembered her mother with love tempered by time, and now at twenty did not know that she acted exactly like her, his long ago Rachel.

From Rachel she had inherited the dancer's body, the head full of curls, the large eyes and the no-nonsense disposition. Solomon considered her beautiful, though she had always thought herself plain.

Perhaps it was that, together with her disposition, which finally discouraged every man that had shown an interest in her. Solomon was certain she was still a virgin, and often despaired of ever being a grandfather. Yet he opposed her intention of staying in the army after her obligatory two years of service were over, even though she seemed to take to army life, the discipline and rigor balancing her outspoken nature. She said it would be easier to find a man if she were constantly surrounded by thousands of them. He found no humor in her jest.

He had argued that his grandparents, as well as numerous aunts, uncles and cousins, had been killed in the Holocaust, that his own father had been killed in the '57 war, and he himself wounded in the Six Day War. She had laughed so hard at the last argument that he finally remembered—Rachel had told her as a child how he had broken his ankle jumping off a truck and missed the whole war by six weeks. When Rebecca had regained her composure, she informed him in no uncertain terms that her decision was not open to discussion, and walked out of the room.

Solomon was constantly worried about her, but he knew she would not accept that as a sufficient reason. When her tour of service was completed and she chose not to return to active duty, he did not question her. She seemed angry and withdrawn since coming home, but whatever happened to change her mind, he was grateful for her safe return.

He blamed himself for not spending more time with her as a child. He thought he should have remarried, that another woman in the home might have softened her, but now it was too late.

She was his daughter, the only person he now loved in this life, and so Solomon forgave her everything, accepting even her scold-

ing with such good humor that the love he bore his only child over-
flowed her anger.

He knew that she was a headstrong and capable young woman,
just as she had been a willful and disobedient child. A tomboy from
the age of eight, teasing boys, hitting them more often, demanding
they treat her as an equal. It began when her mother died. She
came home from the funeral teary-eyed and angry, tearing the black
dress from her body. He had not seen her cry since that day.

Afterwards, she would not wear dresses, not even to school;
though he bought her ones he thought were pretty in the hope she
would change her mind. She sneered at them and climbed trees,
rode bicycles and horses, and never cried. Yet he could deny her
nothing, even as his own mother had denied him nothing since the
day he was born.

> *Socrates: So then, does there exist, in the*
> *mind of the one who does not know,*
> *things that he does not know?*
> *Meno: Of course!*
> *Socrates: So now these thoughts rise in him*
> *like a dream.*
> —Plato, the Dialogue of the Meno

He was a celebrated birth.

His parents had survived the war in ways they would not tell, arriving in the refugee camp in the late summer of the last year. They stepped down from the crowded Red Cross truck with the others and were immediately surrounded; grim faces and sunken eyes searched for lost relatives among the newcomers; mothers, fathers, grandparents, aunts, uncles, brothers and sisters. They did not look for children. There were no children here, and none had so far returned.

Then they saw that she was pregnant, immense in the print dress, and the faces parted to let them pass, watching with hushed disbelief. The entire camp held its breath, as if to do or say anything now would bring some evil peasant's fortune upon the first child to be born among them.

It was only when the old *Rebbe* stepped forward and shepherded them to their room, when they were out of sight, did Sonja and Jakov hear the multitude of voices murmuring behind them.

They had managed to escape their Russian liberators by theft and bribery—it was his father's favorite story, one of the few he would tell of those days—and made their way to the American zone, finally arriving after many weeks in this resort town some twenty kilometers outside of Munich. The beautiful homes of the wealthy Germans—complete with overstuffed furniture—now served as a refugee camp, the former angry occupants having been evicted without notice. The new American Army Hospital had just been built and Shlomeh Freeman was the first child born there four days later.

Is he well? Is he whole? They shouted the questions up, and to each other, when they heard the baby's cry through the open second floor window of the hospital room.

All three thousand waiting on the grounds below looked up as the *Rebbe* appeared in the window. "A boy! A healthy boy! *Gott zu dank!"*

The cheer was deafening; a roar of joy beyond hope, and astonishment. Men and women wept openly, laughing and embracing, congratulating each other.

In the days that followed, every man and women in the camp would touch him for *mazel,* for luck, bringing gifts of whatever clothing or trinkets they could find or salvage.

The *Rebbe* offered a prayer of thanksgiving for their deliverance, and for the boy child born to them this day.

"I know this moment," he said to Sonja, closing the window and leaning over to peer at the tiny child in her arms. Then he whispered softly to the child, "Shlomeh, firstborn . . . The whirlwind passes, another comes . . . And the hidden shall be revealed. Do not fear it." The strange words were more an incantation than a blessing, and then he touched the baby's forehead with the thumb of his right hand.

Jakov looked at the gaunt, bearded old man as if he were mad, but the intense sincerity of his dark eyes touched some deep understanding in Sonja.

"You are Hassidic," she said. It was not a question.

"Shhh," the *Rebbe* whispered, but he was looking out the window at the clouds of a gathering storm.

The boy sits quietly in the book-lined study. He is four, and does not know why his parents have brought him here. Why have they left him alone with the old man whose beard is so long, that everyone calls *Rebbe*? This is not the *shul*, the synagogue. He can barely hear his parents talking behind the closed door. They are waiting in the hall. He wants to run and sit in his mother's lap, but she herself told him to wait, that they would be just outside. As long as he can hear her voice he won't be afraid.

He begins to fidget in the enormous chair when he sees the old *Rebbe* stand up. He was looking at something in an old book and now *he's coming to get me!* He looks like a bear with that beard and the long black coat and wide black hat.

He bends over the boy like a cloud, his voice deep and scary. But he is smiling.

"Now, Shlomeh, I will tell you a story," he says. " One you will remember."

The boy is sitting at the kitchen table in the small apartment. Only his mother is there. She smiles at him as she serves the sweet cabbage soup and dark bread. She calls him *tattala* and kisses his cheek.

"Eat, *tattala!*" she says.

How beautiful his mother is, and so young! He opens his mouth to tell her how much he loves her, but she hushes him. "Eat, Shlomeh! Finish your soup."

He eats, looking at her.

"Shlomeh, what did the *Rebbe* say to you?

The boy is silent.

"Well?"

"A story. I don't remember."

"Eat." she says, looking at him. "I will tell you another story."

He looks at her as she tells him the story of his birth, of the celebration in the refugee camp and of the *Rebbe*.

"He was there with us. It was he who blessed you in the first hour after your birth. And later, when he knew he was dying, I took you to see him when he asked it.

"Finish your soup, Shlomeh. I made it special for you, so you would not be afraid." She sighed. "I did not understand the *Rebbe* then, and he would not explain. Your papa thought he had gone a little crazy from the war."

She leaned over and held his little hands in both of hers. She kissed his cheek and whispered in his ear, "But he was right, Shlomeh. Seek shelter! The whirlwind comes for you!"

The dream woke him. He sat bolt upright in bed, his breath coming in shallow gasps. Tears wet his cheeks, mingled with night sweat, soaking the pajama collar. He ached with the memory of his mother, seeing her clearly in his mind's eye; hazel eyes, smooth pink skin which hardly seemed to wrinkle as she aged, and soft red hair that had only begun to turn gray at seventy when she died.

He washed his face and sat for hours in the chair by the window, completely awake, watching the moon set with distant eyes. He ran his hand repeatedly through the reddish gray bristles of his close-cropped hair, feeling vaguely frightened and prophetic, as if fragments of his genetic memory had broken free of its helix and floated into REM sleep.

The lingering echo of his dream bled into what he had finally transcribed of the young Captain's ancient papyrus, opening his mind like a flower. He shuddered at the desolate places and terrible energies awaiting him.

He must convince his daughter somehow. He could not hide it from her, and he knew she would not be left behind. They must all go see *Shaykh* Haadi about the hexagon cipher. Captain Simach would be arriving in the morning and he must also be told just what it was he found. He will see the necessity. It is irrefutable.

We must go into the desert!

> *Like our bodies imprint,*
> *Not a sign will remain that*
> *we were in this place.*
> *The world closes behind us,*
> *The sand straightens itself.*
> —Yehuda Amichai

Aaron Simach, Captain of the *Mossad*, began to wonder if he was the same man who had walked into the desert. He looked the same, only wearier than he could ever remember; the face that stared back at him in the mirror seemed older every hour, and the eyes now contained a peculiar depth, as if they held knowledge that he did not.

God! What's happening to me? He said to the face in the mirror.

He had been put on extended leave. The Colonel had been sympathetic, telling him to take as long as necessary. How understanding and solicitous he had been. *He thinks I got lost in the desert, like some fool!* He felt like crying, but he did not.

The mission had been a disaster. Intelligence was completely wrong! He and two other young men under his command had joined a group of French archeologists at a small dig near the *Haggar* Mountains. Each man was chosen for his knowledge of the language and the subject, and they had fit in well with the varied group of students until the night came when the three drove the jeep many kilometers into the desert. His orders were to reconnoiter a suspected smuggler's camp, but it had been recently abandoned.

Bad luck from the beginning. They had left the jeep and walked in three separate directions, each in a wide arc that would cover as much ground as possible, looking for anything that would indicate the passage of men.

Who could have foreseen a sandstorm that appears out of nowhere, without warning, like some biblical retribution? Weather radar had nothing on it. *Nothing!*

At sunrise, as he was returning to the jeep, the storm came upon him. It was just suddenly there. The force of the wind hit him like a hand, knocking him over. He landed on the crest of a dune and slid halfway down. Turning sideways, he struggled to get to his feet, but the wind abruptly shifted and pushed him back. He could make no headway no matter how hard he forced himself against it. Finally, he was thrown off his feet, landing against an outcropping of rock exposed from beneath the desert sands by the storm.

He pulled his slicker out of the pack, wrapped it around him and huddled against the rock. Cursing his luck, he clung to the rock, intending to wait out the storm. But an inexplicable weariness overtook him immediately and his eyes began to close even as the storm raged. He struggled against it, pinching himself and slapping his face, but he could not keep his eyes open.

This is impossible! he thought, and with a real sense of surprise he fell asleep.

He woke after the storm with a strange dream fading out of memory. The sand nearly covered him. He dug out of it, the energy of his movements helping to clear the fog in his mind. He stood slowly, testing his limbs, then stretched, shaking off the lethargy in his muscles. He checked his equipment. The canteen was gone and his wristwatch was broken, shattered somehow, but the compass was intact and the sun was directly overhead. High noon. He turned full circle. Only sand and dunes lay in every direction, stretching to the horizon, except for the weathered rock upon which he stood. He walked around it.

It was many meters in diameter, possibly the tip of a massive formation. In a small cave exposed in the rock face, Captain Simach saw the skeleton. It was sitting with it's back against the granite, it's legs outstretched, the elbow of the right arm resting on a boulder, its curving, fleshless fingers almost bidding him to enter. There was nothing else, not even the tattered remnants of cloth hung from it.

He stared at it for a long time in the half-light of the cave. Fine dust swirled impossibly within the eyeless sockets, as if they had a life of their own, and into the nostril holes and out of the lipless mouth like the breath of a ghost.

He did not remember how long he stood there. He felt no fear. He saw the dusty cylinder in the curled fingers of the left hand resting on the floor of the cave. He reached for it without thinking. It was heavy. He ran a finger along its length and saw the yellow sheen where the dust had been. He knew it was gold.

Is it a tomb?

He felt chilled and uneasy. He placed the cylinder carefully in his pack and retreated from the cave, fighting the sensation of the empty sockets watching him leave.

He walked for hours heading northwest, the direction from which he had come and where the jeep should be. He knew his men would wait for him. Finally he saw them in the distance. They were riding in the jeep, circling to the west.

"Haiya!" one man shouted, spotting him and firing a pistol in the air.

He heard the relief in that shout and waited for them, believing their worry was because of the storm. He embraced each of them and accepted a canteen handed to him. He drank slowly.

Silence.

He saw them exchange looks.

"What is it?" he asked. "Did you find anything?"

The senior man spoke. "Uh, no Captain. There was no trace. We were looking for you."

"Ha! What's the matter? Did you think I got lost?"

"Well, after the first day . . ."

"The first day? What do you mean?"

The man shifted his weight from one foot to another, looking uneasy. "You've been gone nearly two days, Captain." He shrugged. " We thought you . . . well . . ."

At first, he could not grasp what they had told him. He was astonished when he finally understood that he had been gone not one day but two. *An extra day! Did I sleep for thirty hours?* He did not believe it, but he could not remember. His mind found the loss bewildering, unfathomable.

He was silent on the ride back to camp. He did not mention the cave or the cylinder. He tried to remember the dream in the sand, but could not. He visualized the cave and the skeleton; the breath, the dancing wind behind the unseeing eyes.

It came upon him then. He felt it begin with a sense he could not name, a whisper just beyond hearing that echoed in his mind, like a voice lost in the wind. He felt the weight of the cylinder in his pack and wondered if the time he had lost was waiting for him within that dream, just beyond the edge of memory.

The feeling haunted him still, days later. Well, soon enough he would know what he had found. In a few hours he and the Professor would both know, and then he could rest. The thought should have pleased him, but he found no solace in it. A sense of foreboding would not leave him, as if the storm had unearthed Pandora's box, and some ancient and terrible curse was about to be loosed upon his head.

I hope it is a grocery list, he thought, but knew in his bones that it was not.

THE MASTER

The greatest knowledge is the one accompanied by fear.
—*Kitab al Hakim* (the Book of Wisdom)
by Ibn Ata Illah

We had listened with full attention to the tale. Indeed, none seemed weary, though we had not stirred since the dawn nor rested since the previous night. The Master must have infused us with some portion of his enormous energy, and perhaps something more; I felt a strange kinship with our guests, as if the unfolding of their private hearts had also opened ours to them.

The Master sat with head bowed and eyes closed. After a moment he looked up.

"Let us see the transcription," he said.

Professor Freeman removed two folded papers from his jacket pocket and handed them to the Master, who read both slowly and at length, and then handed them to me. Ali and Rami leaned in and we read them together.

It was not a grocery list. It was this:

In the name of God, who created heaven and earth.
I, Zadok, son of Ahitub, high Priest of the Temple of God, write this
for Solomon, the Great King, son of David the King, to guard him
against every peril of the way. Heal him of every hurt and infirmi-
ty. Protect him from every demon. Blessed art Thou, O Lord our
God, who hast sanctified Thy great power and might in the writing
of it, and in the utterance of the mouth. Blessed art Thou O Lord,
Holy King, who's great Name be exalted.

And on the second was written:

Blessed art Thou O God exalted be Thy Name
Thy mercy reveals the hidden. The ring abideth.
I pour out my spirit. I will make known my words.
Come O evening star.

We looked at each other in amazement. The Master, who had waited for us to finish reading, now motioned for us to keep silent.

"You are certain it is authentic, Shlomeh?" he asked.

Professor Freeman nodded. "It's authentic. There is no question of it. My laboratory vault now contains one of the most valuable written documents on earth."

"And so you think . . . what?"

The Professor looked out the open window to the sky, his face unreadable, and then shrugged.

"I think Zadok, the High Priest of the Temple, wrote this *kemi'a*, this talisman, to protect the King. It was a common practice. Solomon must have carried it for many years because Zadok died relatively early in his reign. So he would have had it with him if he had become trapped in a desert cave and needed something to write on. And I believe Solomon himself may have written the second part. It was on the reverse side of the papyrus."

"Why do you believe so?"

"It is written in a different hand."

"That proves nothing. How would Solomon come to be so far into the western desert?"

The Professor sighed. "That is only part of the mystery."

70

"Go on."

"Well, historical evidence is sketchy, at best. The Old Testament relates that Solomon took the daughter of Pharaoh as one of his first wives. Psusennes is believed to be the Pharaoh of that time. I have always suspected that Shishak, who became the next Pharaoh, was their son. And if that were so, he may have hated his father. He would have been the firstborn, yet had neither honor nor respect. He was not a Hebrew because his mother was not.

"The First Book of Kings states that, because Solomon had forsaken the commandments of the Lord, after his death God divided the kingdom between Jeroboam the son of Nebat, who ruled over ten tribes, and Rehoboam, the son of Solomon, who ruled over only two from Jerusalem. Shishak even sheltered Jeroboam in Egypt from Solomon's wrath. Perhaps in his old age, Solomon wished to reconcile with his elder son, or prevent the wars he knew would come. Whatever the reason, it was not to be, for in the Second Book of Chronicles it is written that Shishak invaded Israel in the fifth year of Rehoboam's reign, taking away the treasures of the Temple and the King's house. He apparently took everything, even the shields of gold which Solomon had made."

"But not the ring," the Master added.

"Yes, you understand! The papyrus suggests that Solomon had some ring of great value with him. Perhaps even the seal ring."

"Ah! You mean the ring with which he is said to have commanded both men and *Jinn*," said the Master.

The Professor chuckled. "Well, I doubt if it really had that much power. But if he did indeed use a seal ring, he might have had it with him, even in Egypt. He may have been fleeing Egypt so that Shishak could not use him and his ring against Rehoboam."

"Hmm, perhaps." The Master appeared thoughtful. "Or he may have been going to the land of Sheba before he died, to see it's Queen and the son she is said to have borne him, if it is indeed the same ring, and if he took it with him. What you are really saying, it seems, is that Solomon was not buried in the city of David, as it is written in the Old Testament, but went in his old age, for some unknown purpose, into the western desert, and it is his bones that were in the cave."

We looked at Captain Simach and then at each other. Again I felt the chill on my spine.

"Exactly," the Professor said. "Whatever the true reason, Solomon was apparently somewhere near the Haggar Mountains. They are to the far west of Egypt, but Egypt was a larger and more powerful kingdom in ancient days, and many surrounding tribes and kingdoms may have paid it tribute. Perhaps even *Sabia*, or Sheba if you will. How he came to his end so far into the western desert I don't know, but a sudden sandstorm may have buried him in that cave. Then he added those final words to the *kemi'a* and resealed the case with a flat stone, the *bulla* I found on it. And there he remained for nearly three thousand years, until Captain Simach met another sandstorm in the desert."

"Why do you think the words were written after Solomon, if it is he, was sealed in the cave?"

The Professor shrugged. "They were written in blood."

There was silence for a time. Captain Simach seemed lost in the possibilities of what he had discovered, and I was an abundance of questions, but all waited for the Master to speak.

"What brought you here then, Shlomeh? This riddle appears to be within the grasp of even my worst student. How may I help you?"

The Professor smiled at the jest, but his eyes took on the gleam of a magician who has saved his best device for last.

"The original has something more," he said, and removed another paper from his pack, unfolded it, then placed it on the carpet for all to see.

"I copied and enlarged this from the original. It was also on the reverse side of the *kemi'a,* affixed in the same blood. You see?" He pointed out the contents. "Two concentric circles enclosing a hexagon star: The shield of Solomon. This, I believe, is the actual imprint of his seal . . . King Solomon's ring."

He paused, glancing at our stunned faces with a look of utmost satisfaction.

"And you see here," he said, turning to the Master, " these marks within the center of the star. They're barely visible, but I am certain it's a word. Some edges remain, though the letters are so filled in that I needed a microscope to see anything at all. The viscosity of the *ink* used has, well, *bled* into them."

He threw up his hands. "I used the best equipment available for such work—x-rays, infra-red scanners—but the word is unreadable. I don't know why. It should have shown up clearly." He shrugged. "Perhaps it is the hidden name of God. I have no idea. I thought you could help me."

The Master picked up the paper, holding it out and away so that none could see and looked at the unknown word for a moment.

"Shlomeh, if this is the seal of Solomon's ring, and it is also imprinted in the same blood, he would have had it with him in the cave. Why then did he seal the case with a flat stone?"

73

"I don't know," the Professor said glumly. "It is a mystery within a mystery. Aaron . . . Captain Simach, says he does not remember seeing any ring. But you are correct, it may still be there."

The Master regarded his old student silently. There was the hint of a smile on his lips and he nodded to himself before he said: "My friend, why have you really brought this to me?"

Professor Freeman seemed genuinely surprised by the question. "Why? Well . . . Actually, you were the first person that came to mind. I thought it might suggest something to you," he said. "That's all."

The Master sat in thought for some time, stroking his beard while re-examining the ancient words and seal imprint.

"Yes, I see," he said finally, then spoke a few soft words to Rami, who rose and brought him two of the books that filled the shelves on one wall of the room. He read silently from one of them for a moment, the Bible, and then put the volume aside.

"Here is part of the mystery. And you know these words as well as I, Shlomeh. They are from Proverbs. 'Behold, I will pour out my spirit unto you, I will make known my words unto you.' And also, 'For the upright shall dwell in the land . . .'"

"Yes, yes," the Professor said. There was a hint of impatience in his voice. "Proverbs, the one book of the Old Testament which most scholars agree was written by Solomon. There is little question of it now."

"Except that the tense is changed."

"Yes, the papyrus quotation is in the present tense. 'I pour out my spirit.' Solomon was near death, I think." Professor Freeman frowned as he said the words.

The Master said nothing. He picked up the other book and

74

turned its pages until he found what he was looking for and read silently. After a moment he put the volume aside, open to what he had been reading. I could not see its title.

"Yet it seems that even in death and across the millennia, the King may command the living," the Master said. "It is told that when the Queen of Sheba came to visit Solomon, to learn for herself if the reports of his wisdom were true, Solomon sent *Benaiah*, the son of *Jehoida*, the captain of the army to meet her. And *Benaiah* was very handsome."

The Master again picked up the book and read, " ' . . . like unto the flush in the eastern sky at break of day, like unto the lily, growing by brooks of water, and like the evening star that outshines all other stars.' "

He closed the book and looked directly at Captain Simach.

"You see?"

The Captain lifted his head at the words and blinked. He seemed puzzled for a moment, but the distant expression remained. Ali and Rami looked at him in wonder. Rebecca too stared at the man. This was no jest. I turned from the young Captain to the Master and back again.

"Come now," the Master said to his friend. "You also knew the reference. Why did you not speak of it?"

The Professor shook his head. He seemed embarrassed. "Because it's ridiculous," he protested. "This is not science. It's—"

"Yes, quite," the Master said, resting his hand on the closed book. "As unlike science as dreams foretelling the future."

The Professor did not answer, the vision of his mother written plainly on his face. Perhaps the scientist could dismiss the words within that vision, but the son could not.

"What you have told us is quite interesting, Shlomeh, but I am not familiar with ancient Canaanitish, and the message you have already deciphered. This entire matter should have been brought before the Israeli Antiquity Authority. Why have you come to me?"

The Professor hesitated. ". . . I only thought the message might suggest some other meaning to you. It seems like . . . Like some kind of prophecy?"

"You ask what you already know, Shlomeh," the Master said.

The Professor would not be swayed. "But I don't know the word on the seal, or even if it's in the same language. If we can get a sense of *it's* meaning in relation to—"

"That will not help you."

"But, how do you . . .? I mean, how else can we . . .?"

The Professor stopped, at a loss it seemed, or else not wishing to question the word of his old teacher.

The Master said nothing more. At that moment, a small brown moth flew through the open window and began circling our heads. The Master held out his right hand and the moth immediately fluttered to rest on his outstretched palm.

"He seeks the light, even as you," he said, closing his hand gently and placing it in a pocket of his robe. When he withdrew his hand, it was empty.

"It is your dream that has truly brought you here, my friend. But you will not find its meaning here. You already know what you must do. I will help you as I am able, and as God wills."

Professor Freeman looked at the Master's empty hand, at his own hands, and did not answer; his silence more eloquent than words.

"Is there no other way?" his daughter asked.

The Master shook his head. "The truth is not found in books." He then looked directly at Captain Simach. "You must seek the answer in the same place that you found the question."

The Captain closed his eyes.

"Then we must go into the desert," the Professor said.

"Yes, and soon," the Master said.

I knew then that the Master would send us also. It was why we were chosen to remain. Ali and Rami sat silent and unmoving beside me. They also knew.

The Master lit his pipe and closed his eyes for a moment, then looked at Rebecca. Her body had been slumped and her head bowed. Now she straightened and squared her shoulders, looking up at almost the same instant. "Master," she said softly.

Master?

Her voice was gentle, but there was a light in her eyes. "I would like your permission to join the Order."

Professor Freeman looked at his daughter in astonishment, but the Master smiled. He had read her intention.

"This is a matter of the utmost sobriety," he said. "It is a difficult path. The most difficult you will ever know. Nothing of your self will remain hidden. Are you certain?"

She did not hesitate. "I am."

"Your father is my friend. You must also have his permission," he said.

Rebecca looked at her father.

Professor Freeman met his daughter's eyes and shook his head numbly. "I don't know what to say."

"Do you believe in God?" the Master asked Rebecca.

"Oh yes," she answered softly.

"Then you would be welcome," he said. "Among the *darvishes* of the Order are people of every race and creed. We are quite a stew, but all travelers on the same path."

"And will you say the Muslim prayer?" Professor Freeman asked her.

She smiled at him and remained silent.

"Jew, Christian, Muslim," the Master said. "We are all people of the Book, sharing a common heritage. I have prayed with both Christians and Jews, my friend. I assure you there is but one God to hear."

The Professor sighed heavily and bowed his head. The wind blew softly among the leaves and the Master leaned over to whisper in his ear. What he said caused his friend to sit upright.

"Come now! Speak!" The Master said. "The tongue's only customer is the ear."

Professor Freeman shrugged slightly. "Yes, very well," he said, and sighed again as Rebecca put her arm around him.

Captain Simach had not stirred the whole time. The Master turned to him.

"Shlomeh will see his daughter initiated. I would have you here also, so that all voices may be heard."

The words seemed to have an effect on the man. After a long silent moment, his inner thought evident only by the slightest movements of his head and body, he nodded his agreement.

"So be it!" the Master said. "Rebecca will not return to her home. All of you, if you will honor me once more by being my guests, will also sleep here. Tomorrow evening is *majlis*, our twice-weekly gathering. Ishaq will then help Rebecca prepare for initiation."

With that he rose and we rose with him, and as he walked from the room the energy that had sustained us through the long night seemed to be withdrawn. I had barely enough strength to bring the extra mats and blankets to the guest rooms before I fell into the deepest sleep of my life.

Master of the Jinn

> *I drank glass after glass of Love;*
> *neither did the wine finish, nor my thirst.*
> —Bayazid Bistami

The Master himself woke me. This was so unusual that I became immediately alert.

"Make notes of all you have seen and heard," he said. "My old student and his friend shall soon go into the desert, and you will go with them as my scribe."

He must have seen the look in my eyes, for he smiled and added: "Do not be afraid. Ali and Rami will go with you. They know the desert. Rebecca also will go. She knows her father. Hurry now and wake them. The circle is nearly complete."

The circle is nearly complete!

It was true then. The root of the word scribe is *sfr,* which means to count, but it was no bookkeeping function the Master required of me. I was to account for all that happens, to *bear witness.* The old skeleton and cryptic words might be reasonably explained, and even the great seal ring may still exist in some cranny of that desert cave, but we were being inexorably drawn to that ancient enclosure by supernatural circumstances; unearthly winds and impossible resemblances, dreams and blood.

Despite my foreboding, I felt compelled by the mystery of it, as if the Master's words had somehow drawn me into that circle nearing its completion. I trust my Master's eyes, and whatever destiny he had read in Solomon's blood and Solomon's bones was in some way woven with the young man and the old. And we were to share it, Rebecca and Ali and Rami and I.

And so, when the others had been awakened, I sought to prepare our new sister.

I liked her strength and quiet manner; she was not yet a *darvish* and had already learned silence.

She greeted me with a warm smile when I knocked on her door, and I bowed, my right hand over my heart. How calm she seemed, far more certain than I had been before my own initiation.

We had slept most of the day and it was already approaching evening. The other *darvishes* had still to arrive, and those who had been with us through the night had not yet come down, so she kept me company as I prepared the tea for our very late breakfast.

She sat perfectly straight, her back barely touching the chair, hands folded in her lap. I sensed the expectancy in her posture. She was waiting for instruction.

I served her tea and sat facing her, but did not meet her eyes, uncertain of how to begin. I had never done this before.

She read my shyness plainly.

"Thank you for helping me," she said. "I never thought I would be sitting here."

"Neither did I, " I admitted, looking at her, " when I was sitting there."

"How did it happen? Please tell me!"

It was the right question to put me at ease. I smiled in gratitude and told her the tale as we sat at the table in the kitchen.

I first saw the Master through such earnest eyes that I laugh to think of it now. I was quite a serious student then, an outspoken lover of truth and wisdom. You understand? Yes, a philosophy student. Of course, I could afford the luxury of scholarly pursuits. I come from a wealthy family.

Well, one perfect spring day I decided to walk the long way through the park on the way to my rooms, after my last class at the university. There was a small grove of trees near the fountain there and I sometimes stopped to sit and read on the grass. As soon as I neared the grove I heard the music. It was a reedpipe, a *ney*, and I followed the sound into the trees. I thought that some musician had come to practice there, and was surprised to find a large gathering of people sitting on the grass and listening. Perhaps it was a concert, I thought, and looked for a place to sit and listen. The man who was playing was very good. It seemed harmless enough.

It was Ali, of course. Perhaps two-dozen men and women of all ages were seated on the grass, all listening silently. It was then that Rami came up to me. He was in one of my classes, and although I didn't know him well, it was reassuring to see a familiar face. He didn't speak, but he shook my hand and took me by the arm, leading me to a spot in the back and sitting beside me. Unfortunately, it was not very long before the music ended.

"I've come too late," I said to Rami.

"Oh no!" he said. "You're just in time."

It was exactly at that moment that the Master walked into the gathering.

He was really quite an imposing figure as he walked through the trees, dressed in white robes and a white knit cap. I could see sandals and white socks peeking out from under his robes as he sat on a lawn chair facing us.

Rami whispered to me that *Shaykh* Haadi was a Sufi Master, one of the most renowned spiritual teachers of our time, and was himself surprised that he had decided to speak in the park, in public, something he rarely does.

I didn't know what he was talking about, of course. I had never heard of him. Obviously I had been drawn by the music into some kind of religious sermon, and now I felt foolish and self-conscious about just standing up and leaving. I was trapped, and knew I would have to endure it.

Well, perhaps it wouldn't be too bad, I thought. He smiled warmly when he greeted us, and was not at all the solemn figure I would have envisioned.

Shaykh Haadi then put his hand over his heart and bowed to his small audience from the chair.

"Salaam!" he said.

His deep and resonant voice surprised me. It filled the grove as he began to speak of Love, and the long path that leads to God. You've heard him. His voice carries such authority that it gives his words tremendous power.

I felt immediately uncomfortable.

Rami and the others listened with rapt attention, but I had always viewed such mystical poetics with suspicion, no matter how deeply felt. It was not, if you will, my cup of tea.

There was a great deal of applause, but I remember only the last of what he said that day. Oh yes, I remember that very well:

"Friends!" he said. "Your fortunes are not in the stars, but in the hands of *Allah*, the Merciful and Compassionate. Trust in God, and keep the Love of God in your hearts, and your way shall be blessed."

More applause greeted him, and I too applauded politely, relieved that he had finished. I was about to get up and leave when he rose from his chair and held out his right hand. There was a coin in it.

"You see?" he added. "Once, when I was a young man, I went on the *Hajj,* the pilgrimage to Mecca. It was a journey of a thousand miles from where I lived at the time, but I took only one coin in my pocket, for I trusted in God to guide my steps on the way. And when I returned, the coin was still in my pocket."

Everyone was charmed by this tale. Many shouted out various names of God. I couldn't believe it. A scholar's indignation arose inside me, and stirred an impulse to logic I could not resist.

"Excuse me," I said, standing up to face him. "But if you had truly trusted in God, you would have not taken even one coin."

There was an instant of silence, and then a collective gasp. I wondered if I had gone too far. Rami turned to me in shock, and the others looked equally horrified, but *Shaykh* Haadi only laughed. He smiled at me and bowed.

"You are quite right," he said, putting the coin back into his pocket. "I was an ignorant young man."

The others came into the kitchen then. They greeted us and Rebecca kissed her father. He whispered a few words to her and she nodded. Rami poured tea for Ali, the Professor and Captain Simach, then looked at the two of us and led the others into the garden.

"What happened then?" she asked, when we were once again alone.

I shrugged. "He took me aside and asked me to come for dinner the next night. He said that his *darvishes* could benefit from my wisdom."

Rebecca laughed and I did also, though not as much.

"He baited the trap and you walked into it."

84

"Yes," I agreed, and felt on the verge of tears, surprised at the emotions the memory stirred in me.

Rebecca understood. "You didn't really believe in anything did you?"

I admitted that it was true, though I would not have admitted it at the time.

"What happened?"

"The next night Rami came to my room and drove me to dinner at the *khaniqah*," I said, turning my head to indicate the meeting room. "By then I was rather sorry I had accepted the invitation. I thought they would purposely ignore me because of the disrespect I had shown their Master the previous evening. But everyone welcomed me with great warmth and courtesy. I swear I have never met such generous and open-hearted people. Even the Master seemed delighted to see me. He had me sit at his right hand during dinner and spoke at length of the Path, answering patiently my questions on the history and lineage of the Order. I was actually surprised and quite pleased by the attention he showed me, and resolved to repay his kindness by writing a scholarly study of his methodology."

She laughed.

"It's true. I must have looked like a complete fool, scribbling notes furiously as we sat after dinner in the garden. I did not know then the worth of such attention.

"Soon enough, tea and sweets were served. The Master had excused himself and gone up to his room, but Ali began to play his *ney* and the other *darvishes* sang a song of the names of God to the beat of the *dafs*. I think it began then. I had never heard that simple instrument played so, nor voices uplifted in such simple joy. It stopped my pen. I barely remember putting the notebook aside. The music stirred a longing in my heart that I had never known. I remember tears burning my eyes. I couldn't believe it. I kept telling myself that it was all nonsense, but I couldn't stop crying."

I looked away, breathing deeply. The memory held me still, rising out of the depths of that profound astonishment. "I stayed the night, and the next day, and the next. The Master initiated me the following week."

Her brows knitted into silent thought.

"It was just that way?" she asked finally, softly. "Just like that?"

"Yes . . . Though it was more than that also. "

"And have you had any dreams? Any visions?"

"I may not speak of that to anyone but the Master. I'm sorry."

Rebecca nodded slowly, the attentive look fading into acceptance. She stood and poured more tea. I should have been the one to do it, but I rather enjoyed the grace of her movements.

"Well then," she said, after a moment. "Tell me what I need to know."

"Yes, of course," I said lightly, trying not to sound like a scholar. "After dinner we will all be in the meeting room, drinking tea perhaps, and the Master will excuse himself and go upstairs. Then he'll send for you and I will bring you up to him. We will both prostrate ourselves and touch our foreheads to the floor in front of his room. Then he'll call you in. I'll be waiting outside. You must sit directly facing him, and wait for him to speak. Remember that! Speak only if he asks you a question, or gives you permission. What he may ask you, I don't know."

"What did he ask you?"

I shook my head. "That won't help you. It's different for

86

everyone."

She nodded. "Go on."

"Then he will ask what you have brought him."

"What am I supposed to bring?"

"A bag of rock candy—we have some here—and a ring."

"A ring?"

"Yes, a ring with a stone in it. It need not be an expensive ring. We can go buy one if you need to."

"No," she said after a moment. " I have one."

"The giving of the ring is a symbol of generosity. Whether wealthy or not, the *darvish* seeks to empty his heart of attachments to the world. The ring itself is a declaration of your intention. Like the band once worn by slaves, it signifies your devotion to God, and to the Master as your guide on the Path. The stone of the ring represents the head of the traveler. It means consenting to never reveal what may be confided in you."

"What if I have dreams . . . Like my father?" she asked.

"You may tell them only to the Master." I said.

"And the rock candy?"

"It is given as an offering of your second birth. We say that as your mother bore you into the world, separating your soul from God, so you are reborn as a traveler on the Path of Love, returning to God."

"Oh!"

The simple expression touched me. "The Master may then ask you many other questions, or tell you . . . anything. Again, it's different for everyone. Lastly, he will give you a *zekr*, a word or phrase that is a remembrance of God. It is to be repeated silently with each inhalation and exhalation of the breath, so that slowly, after a long time, the remembrance becomes a part of your breathing. Finally, it flows directly from the heart, and then every breath is a prayer, a blessing, and a thanksgiving."

Her eyes sparkled at the image, and I smiled at her in acknowledgment. "After the Master has initiated you, he will kiss you on both cheeks. Then he will return the rock candy after taking a piece for himself. At last, he will call me in and I'll lead you back downstairs. All the *darvishes* will stand when you enter, and you will give them each a piece of rock candy and say *'Salaam'* and kiss each one on both cheeks. I will be the last one in the circle."

I took a breath, looking at her.

"And then?" she asked.

I smiled. "And then you will be my sister, and I will be your brother."

I do not think she realized for a moment that she was crying.

"I'm sorry!" she said. "I'm an only child."

I knew then why the Master had chosen me to aid her with the initiation.

"So am I!" I said, offering her my handkerchief. She reached across the table and held the square of cloth, and my hand, in both of hers. The look that passed between us then sealed the bond of kinship I had felt earlier, and more. It was the beginning of a special friendship, even within the circle of the Friends.

> *The Sea*
> *Will be the Sea*
> *Whatever the drop's philosophy.*
> —Fariduddin Attar

And so it was. At the evening meal we exchanged many quick smiles and secret looks of understanding. It seemed to allay her nervousness, though I was not quite certain what was understood. The Master seemed absorbed in his own thoughts and said little. At the end of the meal he spoke a few words to one of the older *darvishes* and went upstairs.

After the dishes were cleared and the *sufreh* removed, tea was served. Professor Freeman and Captain Simach sat together in a far corner of the room, while Rebecca sat next to me, her head bowed.

Out of courtesy, none of the other *darvishes* glanced our way. They had all known this beginning and did not interrupt her contemplation.

Thus we were until the older *darvish* knelt before us and whispered that it was time.

I led her immediately up the stairs and into the small anteroom of the Master's quarters. The door to his room was open and we could see him sitting against a pillow smoking his pipe. Two glasses of tea and a small tray of sweets were beside him.

We both prostrated ourselves before his threshold and I announced that one had come seeking initiation.

"Let the one come forward!" he said.

Rebecca entered and sat facing him. I closed the door.

Only a few minutes had gone by, however, before the door

opened and she came out. Glancing quickly at me, she went into the bathroom. Soon I heard the shower running.

Such a symbolic cleansing is often a part of the initiation, but the water ran for an interminably long time, enough for five showers. She did not look at me when she passed through once more, her hair still wet, and again closed the door.

Perhaps another hour went by before the door was finally opened and she stepped through, walking backwards, bowing as she closed it once more.

The initiation was complete. It had been an unusually long one, but a new *darvish* had joined the companions of the Way, and I stood to greet her.

"Salaam!" she said softly, and held my shoulders as she kissed my cheeks.

"Salaam!" I replied, and kissed her in turn, tasting the salt of her tears. She was crying silently, even as she held the rock candy.

"The clouds must weep before the meadow smiles," I said, quoting Rumi in an attempt to comfort her. "Such tears are considered a blessing."

"I must be a saint then," she said, and we both laughed.

She still had my handkerchief and used it to wipe her eyes. Then we went downstairs.

"Salaam!" I called out, and everyone, including the Professor and Captain Simach, rose to their feet.

I instructed her to begin, as is our custom, on her right, and go counterclockwise around the circle. She greeted each *darvish*, kissed their cheeks, and handed each one a small piece of the rock candy. They put it in their mouths, or held it to use later in their tea, to share in the sweetness. She also greeted Captain Simach in the same manner, and she hugged her father tightly. Lastly, she greeted me again, and gave me the last of the candy.

"Twice welcome!" I said.

She sniffled in reply.

I then led her to a quiet corner, to sit and repeat her *zekr* until the Master appeared.

This is the time of *mohasebeh*, the balancing of accounts. As it is written in the Koran: *"And verily, whether you manifest what is within you or keep it hidden, God will call you to account for it."* Thus we struggle to eliminate the selfish and petty deceits of the ego from our thoughts and deeds, and to balance God's gifts with our service.

After ten or fifteen minutes the Master came down and joined us. All stood as he seated himself on the sheepskin rug, and then sat at his command. He indicated that Rebecca should sit at his right hand, the Professor and Captain Simach next to her, and I on his left. Ali and Rami sat to my left. When all were seated and settled, tea was immediately served to him. He sipped it out of courtesy, and then began to speak:

"O *darvish*!" he said, his piercing glance encompassing all within the circle. "When God created mankind, all of them claimed to love Him, so He created the pleasures of the world, and nine-tenths of them immediately deserted Him, and there remained but one-tenth. Then God created the glory of paradise, and nine-tenths again deserted Him, and only one-tenth of the tenth remained. And then He imposed upon those that were left one particle of affliction, and nine-tenths of these also fled from Him."

The Master paused to light his pipe, sighing with the exhalation of the smoke. "Such is the lot of humanity," he said, "torn between pleasure, hope, and despair. Yet those that remained, that tenth of a tenth of a tenth, are the Elect. They did not desire the world, nor seek after paradise, nor flee from suffering. It was God alone they desired, and though there is imposed on them such suffering and terror that even the mountains tremble, they do not abandon their love and devotion. They are indeed God's servants and true lovers."

Many tears answered his words, and he went on: "To follow the path of Love is indeed to be a servant, to Him and to your fellow creatures, so they may also find their way. Thus came the word of God's Mercy into the heart of Dhu'l-Nun the Egyptian, as it was related long ago.

"And God said unto him: 'If there come to you one sick through separation from Me, heal him, or a fugitive from Me, seek him out, or afraid of Me, then reassure him, or wishing union with Me, then show him favor, or seeking to approach Me, encourage him, or despairing of My grace, help him, or hoping for My loving-kindness, give him good news, or with right thoughts of Me, then welcome him, or seeking to know My attributes, guide him. And if one who is injured asks help of you, give it to him, but if he is doing evil in despite of loving-kindness, then remonstrate him, or if he is forgetful of it, then remind him, and if he goes astray, search for him. For you have I predestined for My work, and you have I appointed for My service."

The words filled our hearts to bursting, and burn in my memory even now. Never had I heard such power in the Master, nor his voice so moving. Many cried *Allah! Allah!* and wept openly in supplication and gratitude.

Professor Freeman held his daughter as she wept, and his own eyes were brimmed with tears. Captain Simach, though, was the greatest surprise. His face and arms were lifted skyward, as if he were beseeching heaven, and he seemed to be speaking though no sound uttered from his moving lips; and his face was contorted as if he were in great pain. The Master leaned past Rebecca and Professor Freeman and touched the young man's shoulder. His hands immediately fell back into his lap, and he bowed his head and was still.

Even as I wondered at this, the Master raised his right hand and the cries and weeping subsided. He called for music, and this night Ali's *ney* was joined by Rami's *tar*, and many others held *dafs*. One of the older *darvishes* even brought out an ancient *tombeck,* a small barrel-like drum made of mulberry wood and goatskin, which is held under the arm.

The *ney* began to sing it's longing, and the strings of the tar softly twined its hope around each phrase. Soon the rhythm of the *dafs* became faster, and voices were raised to the beat of many clapping hands.

They sang one of the Master's poems:

> Hear, O *darvish*, the song of Love
> the unending tale of the heart.
> God whispers "Be!" and infinity
> takes eternal flight.
> Love commands the darkness to depart,
> and the world to arise in light.
> Mountains, seas and stars bear witness,
> The east wind cries out on the wing.
> *La Illaha illa Allah,*
> O Sufi, the universe sings.

Forgive the clumsy rhyme of my translation; the original is more elegant by far. What is lost, however, may be heard in the drums and clapping hands and every voice raised in the driving harmony, repeating the *shahada*, the bearing of witness, that *La Illaha illa Allah*: There is no God, but God.

Ney and *tar* were stilled as the rhythm of drums and hands and voices went on and on, until the very walls shook with it, and every heart beat to it, and each cell of the body sang in joy and remembrance and longing:

La *Illaha illa Allah! La Illaha illa Allah!*

Ten minutes went by, twenty, thirty, until throats were raw and hands were swollen, and tears mingled with the blood of the heart. At last, the Master raised his hand and the drums abruptly stopped on the last beat.

The shouts died slowly away, but many wept and their sobs mingled with the moans of those who had been overcome and were being revived.

In the first instant of silence the Master calmly lit his pipe and began to speak.

"Why do you weep and tremble so?" he asked. "For what reason do you moan and sigh?"

"Allah!" many shouted.

"Indeed!" the Master replied. "God alone is the ultimate source of the heart's joy and sorrow, both the pain and the cure. The soul remembers this as a drop remembers the sea, and so longs the more for that Ultimate Union. All you will learn on the path is but a reflection of that truth, for all true knowledge is remembrance.

94

Thus we polish the heart with tears, that it may reflect only the light of His mercy and compassion.

"So it is, and so it was long ago, when the *Qalandar* met the bandit chief . . ."

So began the Master's last tale. It was an unexpected one, for the hour was late, well past the time of farewell. But we settled ourselves to listen, knowing that the Master does nothing without purpose.

The Master puffed once more on his pipe and said:

"Not so long ago, as time is counted, there came to a certain oasis far in the western desert a *faqir*. He was a *Qalandar*, a wandering *darvish,* who had walked the deserts of Africa and Arabia for many years, seeking only solitude wherein he could remember his Creator and contemplate the Divine mysteries. His virtue and faith, his submission to the will of God, had been rewarded with tranquility of spirit, and his sincerity and devotion on the path of Love was such that the Hidden had been revealed to his heart, and he had become a *Wali*, a Friend of God.

"Now it came to pass that the night the *faqir* wandered into this oasis and lay beneath a palm tree to rest before the midnight prayer, there was, unknown to him, another man under a nearby tree who was also making camp for the night.

"But the other man was a notorious bandit, once the feared chieftain of a band of robbers who had for years plundered the spice caravans and waylaid rich merchants on their way from the coastal cities to the inland towns. The outcry against his merciless raids, however, had at last reached the ears of the Sultan and he had ordered his soldiers to hunt down the band and destroy them. Many were caught and beheaded. Many others deserted their chief out of fear that they would share the fate of their comrades.

"Eventually, this evil man found himself alone. His purse was now empty, every last coin having been spent in escape, and he was a hunted criminal with a price on his head. Even his former allies, those dishonest merchants who had bought his stolen goods, closed their doors against him. They also feared, lest the wrath of the Sultan fall upon their necks. And so he had fled for many days across the desert and come at last to the oasis where, tired and hungry, he sat beneath a tree and cursed his wretched fate.

"Now I ask you, which of these two men is the greater, and which the less? Whom has God blessed and whom has He cursed? No, do not answer! You do not know the answer, for you are not their judge. The Creator alone is the judge of His creation.

"*Munkir* and *Nakir*, however, the angels who question the dead when they are assigned to the grave, looked upon the scene of the two men and sighed. 'Surely,' said *Munkir* 'here at least the true gold may be seen from the false. These two may be judged, though their end is not yct come. God will have the greater, and Satan the less.'

'Alas! It must be so,' agreed *Nakir*. 'True gold is the most rare, and therefore are the fields of heavens spacious indeed, while the halls of Hell are filled to bursting, overflowing even the deepest pits.'

"Now God perceived the thoughts of His servants, and spoke to the hearts of the two angels. 'Verily, thou hast pronounced their just fate,' He said. 'Yet woe unto mankind had I created the world by justice alone. Am I not the Merciful and Compassionate? Behold! I will visit them with sleep and visions that thou shalt know the truth of My creation.'

"Thus the Lord sent sleep and mighty dreams to the *faqir* and the wretched thief. And lo, the *Qalandar* awoke in hell, even into the midst of the great fires of the pit. And the bandit chief arose in Paradise, where he stood among the saints before the very Throne of God."

The Master laid down his spent pipe and sipped his tea. His eyes searched our faces over the rim of the glass.

"Is it mercy to send the worst of man to heaven?" he asked. "Or justice to send the best of man to hell?"

No one dared answer.

"Good!" he said soothingly. "To cleanse the heart of judgment is to discern the Way of Love. And such was the lesson of *Munkir* and *Nakir*.

"For they beheld the *faqir* awaken in the very midst of Hell, and saw that most worthy of men rise up naked as the fires burned his flesh and the cries of tormented souls pierced his ears. Yet he did not feel pain at the touch of the flames, and showed neither surprise nor fear. His thought was only of his Beloved, and no affliction was great enough to sway his love. He sat among the fires and the torment as a *darvish* sits, and in a voice clear and strong he began to sing.

"*'La Illah illa Allah! La Illaha illa Allah!'*

"The fires blazed furiously as the song began and then dimmed to smoldering embers, and the burning mountains trembled at the Holy Name. Now the tormented souls ceased their wailing to listen, for the name of God is not uttered in the pits. Then there was no other sound to be heard but his, and the song went on and on until the very foundations of Hell were shaken, and the damned souls began to feel a spark of forbidden hope.

97

"Surely Hell would have fallen into ruin had not Satan himself appeared, and begged the *faqir* to depart. But the old man would not move, for he had walked many years on the Path of Love, and the Beloved's Will was his will, whether it be paradise or eternal fire."

The Master paused for a moment to again sip the tea beside him. He did not look at us until he began the tale again.

"And what of the thief?" he asked, when the glass was empty. "This chieftain of bandits who was once so feared and terrible, and who had fallen into wretchedness and misery, the fate of all such men in the end.

"God caused the two angels to perceive his vision also, and they saw him rise and stand robed in white, trembling amidst the host of heaven before the Throne of Almighty God. And the angel Gabriel spoke unto him.

"'By the mercy of the Lord, thy Creator, thy earthly deeds are forgiven thee,' he said. 'Come now and be at peace.'

"And now the truth filled his heart, and great wonder, and every veil fell from his eyes; and he saw with a clear sight the Majesty and Beauty of His Compassion, and he wept.

"And the Lord God spoke unto him, and said: *'O man, fear not. For thou canst not fall so low that I cannot raise thee up.'*

"And fear left the thief. He knelt and prostrated himself before his God and wept. On and on flowed the endless tears of his wasted life, until they became the very waters of mercy and would not cease; and the feet of the saints were washed by his tears.

"He would have wept for eternity had not the vision ended and the two men abruptly awakened. Then the thief saw the *faqir* as he stood, and came to him still weeping from the dream. And the *faqir* perceived all that had befallen them and embraced him, and they prayed together at the midnight hour even unto the dawn. Much befell them afterwards, for the thief became the disciple of the *faqir*, but that is all of their tale I will tell.

"And *Munkir* and *Nakir*, who had perceived but the tiniest particle of the unending mercy of God, bowed before their Creator in submission, and in shame of their rash condemnation. For surely beyond the comprehension of men and angels is the Judgment of God."

Many cried at the tale, and Rebecca was weeping openly. Even after the others were silent, she continued to sob as if her heart was broken. Her father put his arm around her and tried to soothe her, but she was inconsolable. The tale had touched some core in my new sister that I did not understand, and my own fears were forgotten in my concern for her. The Master made no move to abate her tears, however, but looked on her with kindness and understanding, finally gesturing for two of the women to take her to her room.

Professor Freeman seemed as perplexed as I. He was near rising and going after his daughter when the Master leaned toward him. He spoke softly, but his words were clear.

"Yes, go and stay with her," he said. "She is grieving for her mother, and the tears have been long in coming."

Then the father's anxiety was also touched by grief. Immediately he went to her, the wailing sounds of her long-held lament hurrying his step.

I remembered the Master's words: 'Nothing of yourself will remain hidden!'

As if he had read my thought he said to us:

"O *darvish!* Remembrance of God is food for the soul. It is a salve for the wounded heart. From the first step, the *zekr* begins to loosen the grip of the past, and slowly, slowly the burdens of the *nafs* are emptied. Bit by bit, the weight of self-absorption and greed and enmity are cast off and left behind, and as the load is lightened, the journey is more swift. Though fear and sorrow may blind you in the beginning, do not despair. Truth is as a bright light come to darkness. The eyes of the heart must open slowly to see."

The gentle words, spoken out of the deep well of his loving-kindness, awakened in me the memory of my own father's untimely death, and I also began to weep. And many others, whose tears had already dried, wet their cheeks anew, remembering other sorrows perhaps, or the love of those lost to time and fortune.

And even in the midst of our sadness the Master looked on us with compassion, and through the window that is between heart and heart flashed the light that separates hope from despair. He began to sing:

O Beloved, Your arrows sting the heart
Unmercifully. Yet I shall ever be
A relentless target
To the golden bow and endless quiver.
Allah! Allah! Allah!
No sorrow has Haadi but You,
No hope but You, no joy but You,
You are the pain, and You are the cure!

Each heart was touched by the tenderness of the song, and

through bittersweet tears we joined our voices to the refrain:

Allah! Allah! Allah!
You are the pain, and You are the cure!

And so it was that by an alchemy older than the stars, our tears were slowly mingled with joy, and our blood was transformed into the most intoxicating of wine. Slowly, slowly, we became as drunkards, reeling and clapping our hands as the elixir raced through our veins from the very heart of love.

Rebecca was also drawn by the power of the song and came quickly down the stairs to sit with us, her father following close behind. She was crying still, yet the release of her sorrow gave her voice strength and clarity.

And we sang of the pain that was born with the creation of the world, and the hope of joy that we may find before its end. On we sang until our tears were exhausted and the Master slowed the song and brought it to an end. It was nearly the midnight hour.

"Allah!" we shouted for long moments afterwards, as blood and breath grew calm and we slowly descended into sobriety. The Master himself then led us in the night prayer.

We stood before the southern window facing Mecca and called upon God, the Merciful and Compassionate. We bowed to His mercy and prostrated ourselves to His will, and as we stood once more the moon shone on our faces, but the Master was bathed in silver light, as if in the very smile of the Beloved.

Master of the Jinn

> *God transforms the heart with blood and pitiful tears*
> *before engraving His mysteries on it.*
> —the Mathnawi of Jalaluddin Rumi

The Master stood at the courtyard gate and bid goodnight to each of the *darvishes* after the prayer, kissing the cheeks of each one and saying to each a few words of farewell. Even his daughters seemed surprised by his tender words when they left with their husbands.

I stood near him with Ali, Rami, and Rebecca. We too had bid our brothers and sisters farewell. I did not know how long it would be before we saw them again.

I dreaded the thought of leaving, and when the Master walked back into the *khaniqah* I was glad to bolt the gate against the outside world and the journey soon to come.

We followed the Master into the common room and found Professor Freeman bent over the copy of the old manuscript, attempting once more to glean some hidden meaning from the words. But he was alone.

"Where is Captain Simach?" asked the Master.

The Professor glanced over his shoulder to a corner of the room and seemed quite surprised to find it empty. The Master nodded, walking into the kitchen and through the door to the garden.

There indeed was the young Captain, clearly visible by the light from the house, sitting on the small stone bench in the semi-darkness among the trees, staring at the night sky.

There was also another man sitting beside him, and as we drew near I was amazed to see that it was the old beggar; the very same *faqir* who had told my fortune the morning I had found the Master sitting on the same stone bench.

The Master chuckled. "Up to your old tricks, I see,"

"Certainly not!" said the *faqir*. "The garden door was open. I found him sitting here, waiting."

"It is time then!" the Master said.

"Yes," the old man agreed.

The *faqir* rose slowly and the Master embraced him. They kissed each other's cheeks and whispered words I could not hear.

The rest of us looked on in amazement. The Master had given no hint that he knew the *faqir* when we first saw him at the mosque, yet they greeted each other like old friends.

"Here is a *Qalander* summoned to guide you on your journey!" said the Master. "Jasus el-Qulub he is called. None knows the way better than he."

Jasus el-Qulub! The Spy of Hearts! That was a sobriquet given to only a few Sufi Masters of the distant past. It denoted not only great spiritual attainment, but also hinted at paranormal abilities.

And he had told my fortune truly!

I found myself strangely relieved to have him as a guide. The Master had all but said he would not accompany us, and I dreaded being without his love and guidance. And *Qalanders* are said not only to be fearless, but also *awliya,* friends of God, and there were few of them left in the world.

Indeed, the old man now wore the rough, patched robe of his station, pulling it tightly around his thin frame as the Master introduced each of us in turn.

"Salaam!" said the *faqir* to Ali and Rami, offering neither hand nor cheek. In courtesy they bowed formally, hand over heart, to return his greeting.

"Salaam!" he said to Rebecca. "And welcome!" She smiled in surprise and returned his greeting in the same manner.

He knew she was a *darvish!*

He then greeted the Professor, who seemed none too pleased by the sudden guest. The *faqir* looked him in the eye for a long moment before finally nodding. "Yes, yes!" he said, but what he was affirming I could not guess.

Lastly he greeted me.

"Salaam!" he said, moving toward me. There was a dry, flinty smell about him, strong but not unpleasant.

"Salaam!" I answered in return, and a faint smile of recognition creased his lips. Those dark and penetrating eyes held me once more, and again I could neither speak nor turn away. The keenness of his glance pierced my heart like a sword, and in that fraction of an instant I glimpsed an immense, burning knowledge for which I had no name. I felt my doubts and fears flow out to him like blood from a wound, and a wild question washed over me like a wave, unbidden and irresistible.

"Are you the *faqir* of the tale?" I whispered.

The Qalander's smile deepened, and his eyes glittered like stars. "No, young scholar," he said. "I am the thief."

I would have stood there forever with my mouth open in surprise, had not the Master touched my arm. It broke the spell.

"Please bring Captain Simach into the house," he said.

The darkness thankfully hid my dismay. *The thief?* I thought, *the thief?* I cursed my tongue for its ignorance as I hastened to help the Professor lift Captain Simach from the bench. His eyes were still turned toward the heavens and he did not resist, walking between us into the *khaniqah*.

At the Master's instruction, we placed him cross-legged in the middle of the room, and sat in front of him in a semi-circle. The *faqir* sat facing him.

"What's the matter with him?" Professor Freeman asked. The Captain now sat with his eyes closed, his head slightly bowed. There was an ineffable expression on his face.

"Let him rest now," the Master said, not answering the question. He seated himself to the right of the young man.

"But he is ill. A doctor should be called," the Professor insisted.

"No physician has his cure," the Master said.

Professor Freeman looked genuinely worried. "What's wrong with him?"

"Your friend found more than a skeleton and a cylinder in that cave, Shlomeh," the Master answered quietly. "The message of the papyrus you transcribed bears a seal. Captain Simach is now also a messenger, but the seal is on his heart."

We looked at the Captain. He seemed to be asleep, or in some deep meditation. Ali and Rami exchanged glances. Rebecca was staring at the Captain and would not look away. There were tears in her eyes.

Professor Freeman saw the pity in his daughter's face. He took her hand and held it. Perhaps he had already sensed the truth of it, or perhaps it was his daughter's tears, but he seemed to accept the Master's words.

"Can't you do something to help him?" he asked.

"He did not come to *me* for help," the Master said. "His message is not for me."

Professor Freeman sat upright. He looked at Captain Simach

silently.

"Only you can help your friend, Shlomeh," the Master said. "The whirlwind comes for both of you!"

He was startled by the words out of his dream. The Master had spoken them calmly, but with a finality that left no doubt.

"But what . . . what can I do?"

"Ask him."

"Ask . . .?"

"Ask him!" The Master repeated.

Professor Freeman looked at the young Captain and swallowed in a dry throat. The Master and the *faqir* both closed their eyes and bowed their heads.

We watched the strange scene in silence, waiting. I was sitting at the easternmost point of the semi-circle, and saw the *faqir* and the Master look up at the same instant.

"Ask him!" the Master said again.

The Professor inhaled deeply and whispered: ". . . Aaron?"

Captain Simach did not move.

"Aaron?" he said again, touching the young man's hand. "What is it? What do you have to say?"

Captain Simach began to stir. Slowly he raised his head. He looked drawn and weary, but his eyes opened. He blinked. The *faqir* then leaned forward, his back curving like the crescent moon, and peered into his eyes.

"Speak!" the Master said.

And Aaron Simach heard the command of loving-kindness. He sat upright, and looked directly into the ancient, unwavering eyes of the *faqir*. His lungs filled in a long, slow breath. He blinked again, and a spark slowly kindled in his eyes. Again, and a tear ran down his cheek.

With a great, moaning sigh he began to speak. The seal on his heart had been broken.

> "*O LORD! O LORD! NOT FOREVER!*
> *MERCY O GOD! THE FIRE DIES!*"

The power of the voice filled the room, the cryptic words resonating as if they had been shouted among mountains.

I trembled at the sound. It was not Aaron Simach that had spoken.

The Master had promised that "all voices would be heard," but who had uttered those words through his throat? I record them truly, but no pen could convey their lamentation. They had been torn from his lips in anguish.

I realized I was weeping, and the others too wiped away sudden tears with trembling hands. We looked at each other and I saw in their faces the same desperate, consuming thought that had come rising out of some unknown locus of intuition: *Hurry! Now we must go!*

But the Master had neither moved nor wept, and the *faqir* still held Captain Simach's eyes as tears now ran down them openly in release, even as the young Captain swooned into the arms of the Master.

For long moments after he had fainted the Master held him and stroked his brow, gesturing for the rest of us to stay seated and remain silent. Finally, he asked Ali and Rami to carry him to his room and stay with him.

"He is sleeping now, and will for some time," the Master said.

The Professor looked stricken and dismayed. "But what was it?

And . . . And what did—?" he stammered, looking helplessly at the Master. Rebecca held her father's hand tightly.

"The King has spoken!" the *faqir* exclaimed.

"Yes," said the Master. "Solomon the King sealed those words in his heart! There can be no doubt. It was his spirit that waited in the cave, his spirit that called, echoing through your young friend."

Professor Freeman looked at the *faqir,* at his daughter, but he did not deny it.

"But what does it all mean? The words . . ." the Professor asked, hesitating, trembling slightly.

"You were chosen to receive it," the Master said. "And to discover the meaning for yourself. That was foretold of you when you were born, and told to you as a child."

"The Rebbe!"

"Yes."

"But I don't remember what he said!"

"Do you not, my friend? Yet you believe the dream of your mother is true, that what is to come is meant for you."

The Professor lowered his eyes.

The Master looked at him with the utmost kindness. "Truth is an attribute of the spirit, Shlomeh, not of memory," he said. "The journey will reveal what is hidden, in the cave and in your heart."

Professor Freeman considered the statement silently, the internal battle within him evident. To see beyond the veil of reason demanded a *metanoia*, a change in perception.

"Why me . . .?" he asked after a moment. ". . . I am a scientist, not a mystic."

The Master smiled at his old friend. "Shlomeh," he said, "when I first began on the path, I concerned myself with remembrance of

108

God. I sought to know Him, to love Him, and to seek Him. But when I had come to the end, I saw that He had remembered me before I remembered Him, and that His knowledge of me preceded my knowledge of Him. His love towards me had existed before my love towards Him, and He had sought me before I sought Him. By God's will is God known, and by His will, Shlomeh, you have been chosen. The whirlwind comes for you."

Solomon Freeman began to weep. His daughter held him.

The Master said no more. He looked at the *faqir,* then rose and walked out of the room so quickly that none of us had time to stand at his going. I heard his footsteps on the stairs, and then muffled words. Ali and Rami soon joined us. We looked at each other and once again I had the heightened sense of urgency to begin. We had declared ourselves ready to journey to a far country, even unto danger and death, and so, apparently, it was to be.

I felt the greatest fear and elation I have ever known.

The Journey

To display the perfection of His knowledge,
He places all mysteries within the desert.
—Fakhruddin Iraqi

> *Thou hast shut my mouth lest I voice the*
> *mysteries, and in the breast Thou hast opened*
> *the door I cannot name.*
> —the Diwan of Rumi

The morning of our beginning was bright and clear and of good omen. Captain Simach was well enough to join us for breakfast. He seemed subdued and thoughtful, but he moved once more with straight-backed military grace, his eyes alert and steady. We were already seated, Ali, Rami, Rebecca and I, when Professor Freeman walked in with him. We rose as they entered and made room for them, and Ali brought two more settings of plates and silverware. Before it was asked, Ali told them that the Master and our *Qalander* guide had left before dawn on some errand and had not yet returned.

We made no small talk. The questions we had were asked in silence. By the *adab,* we may not intrude on another's privacy. After the meal was completed and the dishes were cleared, Rami served tea. We sat cross-legged in the common room, a small semi-circle forming unconsciously around the young Captain.

He looked at us and smiled. "I am very glad to see you all again, and to speak to you with my own voice."

We all laughed, his good humor setting us at ease.

"Truly!" the Professor said. "But how much of the rest do you remember?"

Captain Simach answered without hesitation. "Everything," he said, looking at the Master's framed portrait on the wall. "I remember everything."

112

The Captain's manner surprised me. He seemed filled with some quiet, unnamed joy. I wondered if he was fully recovered from his otherworldly experience.

"Please, if you don't wish to speak of it . . ." Rebecca said, uncertain of her father's gentle urging.

The young Captain shook his head. "No, it's not . . . it was not painful. Only . . . it's difficult to . . . it was as if my consciousness was slowly pushed aside, and strange thoughts began to fill the empty space. At first, I thought they were my own imaginings, that I was becoming, well . . ." he shrugged. "In the end, I could only watch and listen. But I saw everything. I heard everything."

"Were you frightened?" I asked.

". . . Not at first. It was very subtle. And gentle. Almost like a dream. Slowly I became aware of what it was. I refused to believe it, of course. I really thought I had gone mad. I was very frightened then, until I sensed the . . . " And now his voice became low and introspective. "It touched my . . . I . . . I don't have the words to explain what it was like."

"And now?" Ali ventured. "Are you well?"

"I am well," he said, and his smile was reassuring. "I also heard the words that came out of my mouth. I can still taste them on my tongue." He shook his head. "Then he was gone. I felt him go quickly, and my own mind filled the empty place. It happened so fast, I think I fainted."

Professor Freeman put his hand on his friend's shoulder. "You look older," he said.

The Captain seemed serene and happy. "I feel younger."

There was nothing more to be said. We sat in silence until the Master walked into the room. Captain Simach was the first to see

him and he stood immediately. We all hurried to our feet at his cue and turned to greet him. He went to the young Captain and took his hand, looking into his eyes.

"So! You are not still weary?" the Master asked.

Captain Simach laughed. "No, Master."

Master?

Now I understood his joy. He had accepted the mystery, and the Master had tended him.

"Here is a new *darvish*," the Master said. "At his request, I initiated him last night while you all slept."

We stood looking at them dumbly until the Master motioned us forward. "Come! Greet your new brother!"

"Salaam!" we said together and each in turn kissed his cheeks. I was slightly apprehensive at his touch, fearful that some vestige remained of his strange possession, but his manner was straightforward and his eyes measured and certain as he greeted us.

The Professor also moved to embrace him, then held him at arms length and shook his head. "So you *are* mad after all!"

The Master laughed heartily at this, and we all joined in, though I was not certain the jest deserved it.

As we sat around the Master, he informed us that we were to leave without delay. "I have made the necessary arrangements, and sent messages to friends on the way. Can you leave immediately?"

He asked the question only of Professor Freeman. When the Master says to go, a *darvish* goes.

"Yes, I believe so," the Professor said. "I have no classes during the summer. My time is my own. I must see that my home is taken care of, and pack a few things."

"I will provide the things you need, and your home will be seen to," the Master said. "If you will leave the keys."

Rebecca at once handed him her keys. Her father made no comment.

"Quickly then," the Master said. "In one hour I will drive you to the sea. Your guide will meet you there."

"We're not going by plane?" the Professor asked.

The Master shook his head. "No, my friend. You go by ship and by desert, as Solomon went."

There was no argument, and one hour later we were on the road to the sea.

It was a silent journey, each of us lost in our own thoughts until we came to the port. The ship turned out to be an old freighter, gray and well worn by life at sea. She was flying the Egyptian flag and building up steam to depart.

The Captain was a gruff, burly man who was waiting for us on the dock with a scowl on his unshaven face, stalking back and forth in his impatience to get underway. When he saw the Master, however, his manner changed entirely. He hurried forward and, looking slightly embarrassed in front of the rest of us, bowed his head in greeting. The Master shook his hand warmly and thanked him with many kind words for delaying his departure. I swear to you the man actually blushed at the Master's attention, and bowing again he rushed up the steps to give the order to get underway.

I could hear him barking orders at the crew as the Master's eye caught sight of someone above us at the rail. It was the *faqir*. He stood unmoving, looking down at us. They held each other's gaze for an instant, though I could not tell what emotion passed between them. The guide was too far away, and the Master did not change expression.

I have been with him long enough to know that he communicates in ways I do not understand, subtle and beyond words. No *darvish* questioned it. The others were checking their simple gear before boarding and seemed too excited to notice.

"So much the better!" the Professor exclaimed, rubbing his hands together as he examined the unobtrusive ship. "No one will know where we have gone until we are there. Ah, and then the desert, where mysteries are waiting to be uncovered. Perhaps even the greatest treasure of all, King Solomon's ring."

The Master shrugged. "Perhaps, but even the great ring is only a bauble, worthless of itself. The grace of God was upon Solomon, and that grace empowered the ring. Have you forgotten your dream, my friend? You are not simply digging for stones in the desert. The Unseen has set you all in the path of the storm. What you will learn is worth far more than all the treasure beneath the sands."

The path of the storm!

The Professor was chastened by the Master's sobering tone, as were we all. How easy it was to cling to the safety of old *nafs* in the light of rational day. The Master then embraced his old friend. It was the time of parting, and a wave of loss and longing swept over the company. We moved toward him as one body, but he raised his hand for us to remain where we were. His gaze encompassed us and he smiled; and there was only love and kindness in his voice as he spoke in farewell:

"Remember, O *darvish*, the purpose of your journey. Obey your guide, and stray neither to the right nor the left. Turn your hearts away from common jewels. Love of God was Solomon's seal. Seek the true jewel, and be always in quest of the Good Jeweler."

I begged for power and found it in knowledge.
I begged for honor and found it in poverty.
I begged for health and found it in asceticism.
I begged my account be lessened before God
and found it in silence.
I begged for consolation and found it in despair.
—Ali Sahl Esfahani

We were at sea two days in calm waters, bound for Algiers, sleep-ing on the forward deck far from the workings of the crew. Our guide had gently refused the offer of cabins, warning us to stay together and keep to ourselves lest we unintentionally let slip some word of our purpose. It took little effort. That we were with the *faqir*, who seemed to be known to the Captain and some of the crew, caused them for some reason to avoid us, though they treat-ed him with the utmost deference.

The Captain himself brought us our meals, and we were given the use of his private lavatory. We slept in our clothes and ate together and spoke in soft voices. Even when Ali asked for per-mission to play his *ney*, the old *Qalandar* shook his head. Perhaps he thought it would attract too much attention, though he did not explain and Ali did not argue. The Master had commanded us to obey our guide in all things while on the journey.

We were not used to the solitary ways and inner detachment of a *Qalandar*, however. He would disappear for many hours at a time, apparently eating and sleeping in some other part of the ship. Even during the times of prayer he was nowhere to be found, and he would rarely speak even when he was with us, sitting rather in

silent contemplation, his eyes closed, one leg tucked under the other, his hand and chin resting on his knee. Seldom would he even lift his head, and then only to sigh.

I observed him carefully and came to envy those sighs: The length of the path from end to end seemed to be in their longing; they were like a breath of consolation to my heart. We would usually join in the meditation, though Professor Freeman would more often simply sit and watch him. He had begun to have misgivings as soon as he learned where the ship was bound, and he shook his head as we neared our destination. "Shaykh Haadi had said that we would go as Solomon went," he said. "But surely King Solomon would have sailed for Egypt, then gone to *Tanis* in the northwest delta. Why have we sailed this far west?"

No one knew the answer. Professor Freeman may have been correct in his supposition, but the Master had said that the guide knew the way. Only Captain Simach did not appear concerned.

"We have no proofs in any direction," he said politely. "Yet I think we must follow where we are led, and wait and see. God best knoweth the right course."

It was a favorite aphorism of the Master. The Professor and his daughter turned to him in surprise, but Ali and Rami nodded in agreement. Professor Freeman was an eminent scholar, but this journey from its beginning was beyond the realm of scholarship, and there was a quality of knowing certainty in our new *darvish* brother that could not be denied, as if some memory were still left in him that was not his own.

Algiers.

We had arrived just before dark, but the *faqir* would not yet allow us to go ashore. We sat with him in silence, waiting, for what we did not know. At last the Captain approached us, accompanied by two rough looking members of the crew whom I had not seen before. A boy lingered behind them.

The Captain had introduced the boy as Ahmed when we first came aboard, his youngest son. He was a bright-looking lad of perhaps fifteen, sailing for the first time with his father. The three men approached in a circumspect manner, one that brought them as close to the *faqir* and as distant from us as possible. Our guide stood as the men moved near and walked toward them. I followed at enough of distance to hear their words, and I set them here.

"Salaam." the Captain said to him in greeting. "By the Mercy of God, we have arrived safely. You are well?"

"By God's grace and your generosity," answered the *faqir.* "We are in debt to your kindness."

"Alhamdulillah!" said the Captain, bowing slightly at the compliment. "All praise is God's alone. I do not wish to intrude, but with your permission, a certain matter has arisen for which your guidance is our only recourse, O *Siddiq*."

Siddiq? That was a sobriquet given only to those thought of as holy men by the Berber and the tribes of the *Ahaggar* in the southern desert. It was the same title once bestowed on Abu Bakr, the first Caliph, and designates a man of illuminated inner vision, one whose word was Truth.

Siddiq: The Heart of Sincerity. He was being asked to bear true witness, to arbitrate a dispute.

"How may I serve you?" asked the *faqir,* addressing the Captain but looking at the other two men and the boy.

"Sir," one of the men interrupted. "A thing of value was taken

from my sea chest. This man-"

"I am innocent!" interrupted the other angrily. "I saw the chest open and merely sought to-"

"Silence!" shouted the Captain. The two men glared at each other, but did not speak.

The *faqir* peered at them both. All except the boy seemed uncomfortable under the intense scrutiny of his gaze. Finally he raised his hands, palms upward, and nodded toward the accused man. "Your heart is innocent of this sin, at least," he said. "You may go in peace and without concern."

The man breathed heavily in relief. Thanking the *Siddiq* for his just decision, he bowed and hurried away.

It was over that quickly. The *Siddiq* had perceived the truth of the matter and the judgment was final, if not fully satisfactory. The accuser stared at the man's retreating back, his mouth a tight grimace.

The *faqir* turned to him. "Have no doubt! Your shipmate spoke truly. He saw the chest open and sought to close it when you walked in." His voice was kind, but certain. "Say no more of it! Was your trinket of such worth that you would also lose a friend, one with whom you have weathered many a storm? Make amends, O worthy man, that your account may be lessened before God."

The man's features softened at the words. He lowered his eyes. At last, he too bowed in agreement. The Captain then gripped him by the arm and led him away. "You heard the *Siddiq*!" he said. "Come along! After you have made amends, I will help you search for your possessions, or recompense your loss. I want no trouble on my ship."

They disappeared below, and now only the boy remained. The

faqir sat down on a nearby crate and Ahmed sat at his feet, looking up at him in amazement.

"I have never met a holy man before," he said.

"Of that I have no doubt," said the *faqir*.

"Are you also a teller of fortunes, as I have heard?"

The old man shrugged.

"Will you teach me this skill?" Ahmed asked softly. The question made me smile, but the Spy of Hearts now looked keenly into the boy's eyes.

"Your heart already knows another skill, young man, as do your hands and tongue. Two such skills cannot fit in the same body."

The boy was startled by the words. He began to rise.

"Stay where you are!" the *faqir* commanded.

Ahmed sat down heavily and did not move. He was frightened, but I knew the look in his eyes; pride, mixed with stubbornness and secrecy.

"You need have no fear," said the *faqir*, but his eyes held the boy motionless. "Now empty your pockets."

The boy fidgeted as if he were struggling against an invisible grip, his hands moving as if by some other will than his own. He was genuinely dismayed as out came a seaman's pocketknife, a few *dinars*, and a ring.

"One thief knows another," the old man said. "*She* did not ask for such a gift. Why would you then offer it with unclean hands?"

Ahmed's face paled even as his eyes went wide in astonishment. His mouth opened and closed, but he could say nothing.

"Answer!" the *faqir* demanded sternly.

Ahmed could not look away. Tears sprang from his eyes.

"I didn't mean . . . I . . ." His voice was barely a whisper.

"Foolish boy! By the wisdom of God we are ordained to love, even as the particles of the world are attracted one to the other, like to like. But know you assuredly that love is not gained by wickedness. It is lost. Hell is the only reward for a thief!"

Ahmed blinked at the words, very frightened. He could not stop crying. "Will you tell my father?" he asked miserably.

"I am not your judge, nor is he," said the *faqir*. "But *Allah* is the Most Merciful. You must make amends, and then ask His forgiveness. Now go!"

The *faqir* sighed and lowered his eyes. The boy shook his head as if released from a spell. He stood and wiped his eyes, then hurried away without another word. I was also about to return to the others, but the *faqir* stopped me with a look, gesturing for me to come and sit in the boy's place. I obeyed.

He glanced at my notebook. "Write also in your account, O scribe, that his fault was in his method, not his madness. "

"I will," I said. "But what shall I write of the *Siddiq*?"

He dismissed the question. "That is it how I am known to some in this part of the world."

"Have you other names as well?"

"Yes, many."

I wrote as I was instructed, greatly intrigued, but I could not bring myself to press further. For courtesy's sake, and the odd empathy and admiration I felt for the old *Qalandar*, I changed the subject.

"What will happen to the boy?"

The old man shrugged. "Many covet what their hands do not hold, and for lesser purpose. To God alone belongs the Judgment." He shook his head. "Alas for man, for within the awareness of love

122

is hidden the awareness of God, and they see it not. Yet perhaps he will find his way. The crooked foot may still walk the straight path, and fear is often a most worthy guide to the young."

"Should not then every thief fear Hell?" I asked. Instantly I regretted my words, but there was no anger in the strange expression that crossed his face. He appeared distracted, rising and stepping to the rail. The setting sun was just touching the horizon and the sky and ocean were red as fire.

The ancient *faqir* seemed lost in thought for a moment, watching the light slant across the waves as it was absorbed by the sea. His face and beard were turned red as the waters, as if he too were absorbing the light.

Without turning he said, "Verily, God's mercy precedeth His wrath. And I assure you, young scholar, the inhabitants of Hell are happier than they were in this world, for in Hell they are aware of God, and in this world they were not. And nothing in this life or the next is sweeter than the awareness of God." Then he breathed deeply of the sea air, fresh and tinged with dying light. His body shook slightly. It was almost a sigh. "Alas, though their longing is a thousandfold greater than the heights of your *sama*, it may never be satisfied. They are barren. You will see."

You will see! His words frightened me.

Who really is this strange old man? I wondered again. *And where in God's name is he leading us?*

123

Master of the Jinn

Everyone's journey is toward his perfection.
—the Mantiq al-Tayr
(The Conference of the Birds)
by Fariduddin Attar

It was not until well after midnight that the *faqir* allowed us to leave the ship. The Captain and most of the crew had gone ashore hours earlier. Only those left on night watch were still aboard. The *faqir* sat in silence on the deck, immobile, his head bowed. At times he would glance briefly at the stars, then return to his contemplation. At last the moment came when the stars must have been favorable. He stood without a word and walked off the ship. We followed close behind, unseen by the watch and without farewell.

Captain Simach cautioned that it was impossible to leave the dock area without going through Customs. High walls and barbed wire fences blocked every other route. The *faqir* made no comment at this information, and indeed led us directly to the Customs office. For some reason it was nearly deserted. An old woman was sweeping the floor, and the Customs officials normally on duty, even at this late hour, were absent from their desks.

Apparently there were no other ships scheduled to dock, or they had gone off for food or sleep. I expected a long wait for their return, but the *faqir* did not slow his step nor turn his head as we approached, walking past the empty desks and out of the building. We could do nothing but follow, and now he set such a brisk pace that we nearly had to run to keep from falling behind.

"What are you doing?" Professor Freeman shouted at his back. "Our passports and visas have not been stamped or approved. How

will we get out of the country?"

"With God's help," said the *faqir,* without slowing.

"But if we're stopped-"

"We must be in the desert before dawn," was all he would say. He increased his pace and soon none of us had the breath to argue. Only Captain Simach and Rebecca proved equal to the old man's legs, matching his long stride in perfect unison, as if they were on a military exercise. The rest of us fell far behind.

Only when he reached the *Casbah* did the *faqir* slow his step. We came to the shuttered shops and empty stalls barely in time to see him turn into one of the side streets that fed the famous bazaar, with the Captain and Rebecca close behind. When we turned the corner in pursuit, they had already come to a halt in front of an unlit doorway on the dark, narrow street.

At last, I thought, exhausted and out of breathe, but even as we approached I saw the *faqir* enter the door and close it behind him.

"Where has he gone to now?" the Professor asked hoarsely.

"He said to wait," Rebecca answered. Captain Simach nodded.

And so for long moments we stood shivering together as the sweat dried on our bodies in the night air.

"Is this the pace he expects us to follow in the desert?" the Professor asked, coughing.

Rebecca turned to him and whispered to keep silent. He was about to whisper some comment in return when a light appeared at the other end of the street. A door had opened and a large number of men came through before it closed behind them. It was no doubt a drinking or gambling establishment, for in the quick illumination I saw that they were dressed like laborers, and the smell of alcohol reached us even though we were some distance away. Some were laughing and others seemed to be cursing in a strange language. When they noticed us, however, their revelry stopped at once.

For a moment there was an eerie silence between us in the near dark. Then one of them stepped forward and began to speak in a rough and belligerent voice.

It was the same language—*Berber*, I think—and though I did not know what was being said, there was no mistaking the tone. Captain Simach put a finger to his lips, whispering that we must give no answer lest our foreign accents betray us. Our silence only served to excite them further. They began to move toward us, the one who had first challenged our presence leading the way.

Captain Simach took one step forward as Rebecca discreetly pulled her father behind her. Ali and Rami moved to either side of the Captain, effectively blocking the narrow street, and I stepped in front of Rebecca and her father.

My senses became acutely heightened by the danger, taking in the scene as if it were in slow motion. I heard Rebecca having some difficulty restraining her father, and saw Ali and Rami tense their backs and clench their fists in the semi-darkness. Only Captain Simach stood as if he were casually waiting to greet them, with his hands open by his sides, feet set apart and knees slightly bent. My heightened awareness was not fooled; his easy posture was the defensive stance of one trained in personal combat.

And still the men came on, their curses preceding them until they were almost upon us. The leader of the ruffians now shouted in Arabic: "Are you all deaf? Why don't you speak?"

The immediate physical threat sped my mind into real time just as the door beside us opened. The sudden brightness brought the men to an abrupt halt only a few meters away, and the *faqir* stepped onto the threshold with the light behind him.

"Cease your braying, O donkey!" he said, glaring at the leader. "The proper reply to a fool is silence."

The man's angry scowl vanished instantly and his eyes widened in recognition. *"al-Muazzim!"* he whispered, taking a step back.

The word spread through them like a cold, sobering wave. They peered at us now with startled, fearful faces. Some covered their eyes; others made warding signs in our direction. They moved slowly backwards a few paces, then turned and fled. *"Shaitanun!"* some shouted as they ran.

"Come!" said the *faqir*, without a glance at the retreating men. "This way."

We hastily followed him through the doorway and into a courtyard lit by torches, then through another door leading onto a different street. A Land Rover was parked there, its motor running.

"Drive!" he said to Captain Simach. "The southern road is clear and the gates will soon be open."

Three hours later we had traveled swiftly through the Atlas Mountains, taking the most direct of the five great north-south routes across the Sahara, and as dawn approached we passed Laghouat, a small town in the southern foothills. Soon we would be in the heart of the desert. The road was clear indeed; we had encountered few other vehicles, and we had passed no gates, either open or closed.

Ali and Rami had stretched out on the packs we had thrown in back. I sat in the rear seat next to Rebecca and her father. The others slept a little, releasing the tension of our incident in the city, but I could not. And the *faqir* was still in the same position as when we

127

had begun, leaning slightly forward and peering silently into the darkness.

I had begun to feel a real affection for our resolute *Qalandar* guide, beyond even the familiar attraction I had known earlier. My companions, I think, were also coming to trust him. The Master had said that he knew the way, and indeed he seemed the equal of any darkness or danger. The unstamped passports were forgotten for the moment, and his timely acquisition of the Land Rover had not been questioned. "To replace Solomon's chariot, no doubt!" Professor Freeman had said, and we all laughed. The seven travelers, besides any other affinity, were slowly becoming comrades together.

But another piece had been added to the board. The drunken ruffians had named him *al-Muazzim*, and there was no mistaking their fear at his coming.

al-Muazzim: The Sorcerer! One who by the black arts may command evil spirits to do his bidding.

While the others slept, I quietly broke the silence.

"Another of your names?" I asked in a whisper, leaning over the front seat.

"Yes, among the ignorant," he said, not turning his head or shifting his position. "As among them you are now my demons."

I leaned back into the seat and closed my eyes. The journey had revealed glimpses of him reflected in the mirror of many hearts, each determined by the level of the viewer's discernment: *Jasus el-Qulub; Siddiq; al-Muazzim.*

Which of them, I wondered, would lead us into the whirlwind?

The Journey

What need does the chooser of solitude
have to look upon anything?
Since there is the lane of the Friend,
what need is there of the desert?
—Hafez

Ever south we rode through blazing day, passing Ghardaia as we skirted the easternmost rim of the Great Western *erg*. The road was flat and smooth for many kilometers, laid in the hard, rock-strewn remnant of what was once the bed of a mighty river flowing down from the mountains. We ate in the Land Rover and took turns driving, stopping only at the times of prayer to refresh ourselves, and that always off the road and out of sight.

The *faqir* would not leave the vehicle even for prayer, however, and no longer spoke in any tongue, gesturing when to stop and when to begin again. To my knowledge he had neither slept nor eaten, and I had yet to see him drink, as if he now needed only sunlight for sustenance, and unknown waters sated his thirst.

The Arabs call the desert the *Garden of Allah*, from which God removed all unessential life so there would be one place on earth where He can walk in peace. Perhaps that vast outer emptiness had wrapped the *Qalandar* in her inner solitude. Or perhaps our swift journey had rekindled some long dormant flame in him. I did not know, but his eyes now burned with such intensity that I feared to look at him.

The Master had named him our guide and we *darvishes* did not question it, but Professor Freeman was becoming increasingly uneasy.

"What's the matter with him? Why won't he speak?" he asked,

129

when we were next permitted to stop. I think he was concerned for his daughter's safety most of all, even though she was unperturbed.

"He knows the value of silence," she said.

Ali and Rami nodded at her words. Only the ear can gain knowledge, we say. The tongue speaks what it already knows.

"And we are much nearer now," Captain Simach added. He stood and shaded his eyes with his hand, peering expectantly at the horizon to the south, his senses open and alert to the slightest sound or movement, the subtlest shift of air pressure—of storm warning.

Nomads could sense a storm this way, but the wind that was to come was not for them. After a moment he lowered his hand and walked back to the Land Rover. We followed without comment, Rebecca taking her father by the arm. The brave Captain's words had tongues of their own, and they whispered with another's voice of what waited beyond the wind.

Ali and Rami understood our tension and attempted to distract us with their knowledge of the desert landscape. I must admit that I felt a strong attraction to the clean and empty spaces. Not that the Sahara was truly clean or empty, they pointed out. Mountains form its spine, and gravel plains, called *regs*, surround the mountains, where once great rivers flowed. Life abounds here in many forms, each particularly adapted to its world. Only the *ergs*, those great sand seas that rim the mountains and the plains, are true desert. They cover a quarter of the Sahara, but even there occasional rain collects between the dunes, and tufts of *aristida* grass and *had* bushes feed both addax antelopes and the camels of passing Nomads. Ali pointed out a long-eared *fennec* fox, the smallest of its species in the world, hunting a mouse-like *jerboa* that had strayed from its nest beneath the thorny bushes.

My *darvish* brothers knew the desert, its ways and creatures, and explained each fleeting shadow we glimpsed from the road. I delighted in their knowledge and made careful notes, Rebecca reading over my shoulder. Captain Simach was again driving as we left El Golea, where we had stopped only long enough to purchase fuel and supplies and refill our water bottles. The sun had nearly set and the terrible heat of the day was quickly dissipating as we approached the *Tademait Hamada*, a high desert plateau north of Ain Saleh.

The *faqir* motioned for us to leave the road as it lifted onto the plateau, directing Captain Simach by hand gestures until we came to a narrow valley that had been carved out of the sandstone rock by the retreat of the same ancient waters that once had covered the desert. Under the slope of an overhanging cliff he signaled us to stop, just as the sun was setting behind a ridge to the west.

There was a small *guelta* there, a rock-pool hidden in the crevice of huge boulders near the cliff-face. Ali said there were hundreds of such pools spread across the desert, and that many forms of life depended on them, including the Nomad tribes during the dry season.

I wanted to explore the many tracks I could see around the pool, but the *faqir* emerged from the Land Rover immediately after the sun went down and commanded us in a stern voice to make camp beside a shallow cave near the rock pool. We were so shocked to hear him speak again that it took us a moment to begin. Even as we set to work, he disappeared behind the rocks.

"Now where's he gone to?" Professor Freeman asked, though I think he no longer expected an answer. I helped Rebecca unload our supplies as Ali and Rami gathered stones to build a low wind-break across the front of the cave. It would be a long, cold night.

The last of the light had faded into darkness when the *faqir* returned with a bundle of firewood. Rami arranged it carefully into a large cone and we soon had a fire blazing, our shadows angling in the dancing light.

Rebecca and her father prepared the evening meal of fried eggs, bread and cheese, setting it on a small *sufreh* the Master had given her for our journey. And remembering always the *adab*, the *faqir* passed the food from right to left until all but he had taken a portion. None commented on his abstinence as we thanked the Most Bountiful for our sustenance and our safe passage. Professor Freeman, caught in the moment, even intoned the Hebrew prayer over the bread, to the delight of his daughter.

"You haven't done that in years," she said, kissing his cheek. He grumbled something under his breath and we all laughed at his feigned petulance—all but the *faqir.*

"Indeed!" he said. "If you do not thank the Provider, what provision will he give you?

The Professor did not answer.

When the meal had ended and we had again given thanks, Ali stoked and replenished the fire. The temperature had dropped quickly and it had become very cold. The *faqir* opened a compartment under the rear floor of the Land Rover and brought out a large bundle wrapped in brown paper. Untying the string, he handed each of us a flowing blue cloak of the kind worn in the desert by Tuareg nomads. Called a *gandura*, it was a hooded protection against both wind-blown sand and the cold desert night.

"Where did these come from?" I asked.

"The *Qutb* has many friends," he said, sitting near the fire and closing his eyes.

We slipped the desert robes over our own garments. Each fit as if they had been measured and cut for the wearer. Ali and Rami praised the Master's foresightedness, and Rebecca swirled the cloak in a graceful pirouette, but Professor Freeman and I glanced at each other and were shamefaced at our many questions and little faith. The Land Rover with the keys left inside had been neither accident nor theft, as we both had secretly thought, but the design of loving-kindness, of preparation and messages to friends. I began to wonder if even the empty Customs Office was not also a measure of service and intention.

We drew the *ganduras* tightly around us and Professor Freeman poked at the fire.

"How soon?" he asked. We all looked at the *faqir*, knowing what was meant by the question.

"One day and one night more," he said. "And the desert will reveal what is meant for each of you."

Captain Simach frowned thoughtfully. "If there has been another sandstorm, the cave may be hidden," he said.

The *faqir* opened his eyes. They shone like polished onyx in the light of the fire. "When God contracts, He hides what He has revealed, and when He expands, He restores what He has hidden."

The Captain's frown deepened. "We're also approaching the area from a different direction," he said. "I'm not certain I can find the exact location again."

"What?" Professor Freeman started to rise, but was stopped by a wave of the *faqir's* hand.

"Have no fear of that," he said. "You did not find it the first time. It found you."

Master of the Jinn

> *The sincere heart*
> *serves as a mirror;*
> *Mysteries are directly observed*
> *through it.*
> —the *Diwan* of Hakim Sana'i

With the dawn we rose and departed into the strangest of days. Once more Captain Simach was driving, and again our guide sat unmoving and silent as we passed through Ain Salah and into the Atakor mountains, the heart of the *Ahaggar.*

I had never seen such a forbidding landscape; domes of granite and crumbling columns of basaltic rock, black and dark gray and rising into twisted, menacing pinnacles devoid of either soil or vegetation, like the bared teeth of the earth. Professor Freeman said the Tuareg call these mountains the "Country of Fear," and I did not doubt him, breathing a sigh of relief when we left the black hills behind and rode into Tamanrasset.

It was quite a large town, once the seat of French colonial rule in this region. We drove slowly through the narrow streets until we came upon the marketplace, where we once again refueled the Land Rover and purchased food and clean water. Without having to be told, we did not stray from the vehicle. The market was crowded and there were other foreigners also moving about. I heard French and German spoken among small groups that passed near us. Some stared curiously at the *faqir* in the front seat, but none approached to inquire after us. Not even the townsfolk ventured near, and I wondered if he was known here by any of his names.

It was not until we were leaving that the *faqir* began to act even

134

more strangely. I was driving at the time and he had motioned us down a wide lane that led south and out of the town. After a few moments he signaled for me to pull over and stop. We were nearly at the edge of town and there was nothing out of the ordinary around us. The sun was low in the sky and the few people on the street were walking to their homes after shopping or their day's labor.

The *faqir* immediately jumped out of the vehicle and approached an unkempt man who staggered toward him, oblivious to his presence: A drunkard making his way home, no doubt. To my horror the *faqir* picked up a stone and threw it at the man, hitting him squarely in the chest. The unexpected blow startled the poor fellow so that he stumbled off in another direction.

My companions and I looked at each other in shock as our guide walked calmly back and repositioned himself in the seat. He pointed south without a word and I sped away. No one spoke after that, though the same doubts and questions radiated from each of us.

And so it was for some hundred kilometers south of Tamanrasset, where we left the main road and traveled east and south along the foothills of the *Ahaggar*, the terrain gradually leveling into the rocky flatness of the *reg*. We were near the Niger border, only a short distance from the sea of *Tenere*, the great sand *erg*. The sun was setting, and the long cumulus clouds of late evening reflected the dying light. This would be our last night before the storm.

We made camp in some nameless *wadi* beside another *guelta*, but our guide did not vanish as he had done the previous night. He sat on the trunk of a fallen tree, watching us silently as we quickly

bent to the task of unloading the Land Rover. I felt the discomfiture of his glance as I collected kindling for the fire.

Professor Freeman seemed less discomforted, momentarily distracted by having discovered a species of Mediterranean oleander growing at the edge of the *guelta,* thousands of miles away from its original climate.

"Strong winds must have carried its seed into the high air currents," he said. It had taken root in the wet sand beneath the rock and formed a green bush covered with small pink and white flowers.

"That I cannot say, but it is one way to distinguish city camels from desert camels," Ali noted with a smile. "Desert camels will not eat the leaves. They're poisonous. But city camels who were not bred in the region don't know that and make themselves ill."

Professor Freeman clapped him on the back. "Well, this city camel is grateful to have a desert camel with him."

The *faqir* nodded somberly at the words. "Indeed! We now have need of a desert camel."

The sun had set and his voice had returned. We all turned to him, but before any of us could ask what he meant, we were startled by the sudden and unmistakable bleating of camels in the distance. Some caravan was also entering the *wadi* to make camp for the night. We looked at each other but said nothing. Rami lit a fire and soon I heard many footsteps approaching us.

Perhaps a dozen men stepped into the light of the fire to find us standing and waiting; all except the *faqir*, who did not stir from his seat on the old tree trunk. I took his calm as a good sign, and so it was.

"Peace be unto thee, Afarnou!" he said to the man who led the

others, "And to thy companions."

"And to you also be peace, O *Marabout!*" said the leader. "And to those with you."

Afarnou also wore a blue *gandura* cloak, though his men did not, and his head alone was covered in Tuareg fashion; wrapped in yards of black cloth so that only his eyes could be seen. But he dropped the veil that hid his face when he spoke to the *faqir.*

And he had called him *Marabout!* The Tuareg name for a holy man! It was the last of his names we were ever to learn, but one.

Afarnou wasted neither time nor words. He was *modougou* of these men, the caravan boss, and he sent them back to their own camp when he had ascertained that we were with the *Marabout.* Even so, he did not seem particularly surprised to see us, although his expression and tone were heavy with suspicion and cynicism.

"My father also sends his greetings. He has placed us at your service, though what need you have of us I cannot guess."

"I have no need of you," said the *faqir.* "Only of one of your camels to carry our supplies in the deep desert, where our vehicle cannot go."

"A camel? But we . . .my father could not have known of this!" he said angrily. "We have traveled many kilometers out of our way to—"

"To be of service. Do so now and be at peace. The promise of bread does not appease the hunger, and Allah is best invoked with the tongue of deeds."

I saw him accept this silently. He would not question his father's command or the word of a holy man, no matter his suspicions. He looked at the Land Rover as if it were some alien artifact whose purpose was unwholesome.

137

"As you will," Afarnou replied coldly. "But you at least should ride upon the camel, if you will not be dissuaded from this foolishness. Others may share the burden."

"I require no ship to sail this sea."

The *modougou* considered this without comment, then turned to examine us more closely. He merely glanced at Ali and Rami, and me only long enough to snort when he saw that I was scribbling in my notebook. He stared at Professor Freeman and Rebecca, however, and especially at Captain Simach, who returned his hard glance evenly and without fear.

"Bone hunters!" he said at last, and I felt my pulse skip a beat.

"What do you mean?" the Professor asked cautiously.

"Pah! Your *ganduras* do not hide your intent, and you are not the first I have seen, sifting the sands and disturbing the bones of ancient beasts, like vultures picking at carrion. Why would my father aid such as you?"

Professor Freeman merely stared at him, but I breathed a silent sigh of relief.

He thinks we are fossil hunters! Paleontologists!

"Well?" Afarnou demanded. "Have you nothing to say?"

When no one spoke, he shook his head and went on, addressing us as if we were foolish children unable to comprehend a simple lesson.

"The Tassili plateau would be more to your liking. There you would find bones and arrowheads, and cave drawings from a time beyond memory. Take your vehicle and go there, for your own safety. You travel too light for a desert journey."

"True, we are not burdened," the *faqir* replied, ignoring the threat in his words. "And we will be no burden to your camel. If

138

you will leave one hobbled at your camp, we will come for him at dawn, and by your father's kindness continue on our journey. Is it not enough that he knows why he aids us?"

"I have no spare provisions to give you."

"We require none. Go in peace and lead your men well."

The *modougou* chafed at being dismissed. Courtesy required that he be asked to stay and share our meal. He looked disdainfully at each of us once more, then turned on his heel and disappeared into the darkness.

Our guide had not stirred at the Tuareg's anger, and did not move even now. He peered into the flames as the rest of us ate in silence.

Afarnou did not wait until dawn to be rid of his obligation. One of his men soon brought a camel into our camp and hobbled him without a word. He then bowed quickly and left immediately.

Rami examined our new companion and shook his head. "He is old and already weary. I doubt he would have survived their caravan."

The *faqir* nodded. "God has granted him a respite for our purpose."

He had Rami move him close to the pool where he could drink and graze, though he did not touch the oleander bush.

Our company had grown by one camel and many questions. After the meal was cleared away, I ventured to ask the least of them.

"By your pardon, O *Siddiq*," I said, invoking the name that bore true witness. "Will you not, as our guide and for our peace, explain the meaning of your actions in Tamanrasset?"

A faint smile creased his old lips at my courteous words. "For

courtesy's sake then, what would you know?"

"Why you threw a rock at that poor man," Rebecca said.

"Poor he was, indeed," said the *faqir*, "a thief and highwayman with blood on his hands. His name is writ large in the scroll of *La*, as one of those who is disobedient to God. Yet he had done a good deed that day, aiding an old blind woman seeking her way to the mosque. Would that he had entered also but his path led him to the tavern instead, from which he lost his way home. I sought to reward him in kind. The stone sent him stumbling on the path toward his home."

My companions and I looked at each other in silence. The language of reason was too poor a judge of his far-seeing eyes. Professor Freeman, however, was far from satisfied.

"Are you saying that you *see* both past and future?" he asked.

"Or was this some vision or revelation you had?"

The *faqir* shook his head. "You confuse prophecy and pre-science, and understand neither."

"Please, I would like to understand," the Professor said.

"You cannot, not in words. Soul receives from soul the knowledge thereof. Only the *Qutb* will avail you on that journey, if you choose to take it."

He turned his eyes to the fire and would answer no further questions. An hour passed with only the quiet breath of our own thoughts. I was beginning to doze when the *faqir* suddenly leaped to his feet and stared intently at the stars. His eyes burned with a wild light as he lifted his right hand to indicate some point on the horizon.

"Arise! The time for sleep is past!" he said sharply. "Too late now to turn aside. The gates of heaven are open." He turned and sped away, vanishing once more into the darkness beyond the fire.

We jumped to our feet, but he was gone. There was no sound even of footsteps moving away in any direction.

"What did he mean?" Rebecca asked, staring into the dark after him. "What gates are open?"

Captain Simach was also looking at the sky but did not answer. Professor Freeman followed his gaze, turning slowly until he had come full circle.

"Why, he must be referring to the gate stars!" he exclaimed, pointing to each distant point of light as we followed his upraised finger. "Do you see? Antares is rising in the southeast, and Vega in the northeast. And there is Regulus I think, or possibly Capella, setting in the northwest, and, yes, Sirius setting in the southwest. At this time of night they each appear at the semi-cardinal points of the compass. The 'Pillars of the Sky' they were once called, and also the 'Gates of Heaven.'"

The Professor clapped his hands at the realization. The sharp sound echoed among the boulders, startling us, and we laughed at our own fright.

"Nothing to be afraid of," he said, putting his arm around his daughter.

"Of course not," Ali said. "All desert travelers know the stars. Their position guides our movement on night marches. See there!" he added, pointing upward. "By following the Female Camel we find the pole star, our guide on the night journey."

Professor Freeman nodded. "The Great Bear constellation in Ursa Major."

"Wait. . ." Rami said, looking puzzled. He scanned the horizon

and the sky, his expression becoming more and more perplexed.

"What is it? What's the matter?" Rebecca asked, trying to follow his gaze.

Rami would say no more. He looked at Ali and nodded. They sat together by the fire and began to softly whisper their *zekr.*

"What's the matter? What did you see?" Professor Freeman demanded, standing over the two cousins.

But it was Captain Simach who answered. He glanced overheard and sniffed the air. "The stars do not move. They should have set by now. And listen! There's no sound! No animal or bird or insect!" He seemed almost happy. "We have been moved out of time, and the wind has risen. Can't you feel it? Even now, we are within the eye of the storm."

The *Jinn*

A sign of love it is to
throw away both heart and soul,
to cast behind you all time
and place and space;
to be now infidel
and now a man of faith
and abide in both degrees
unto eternity.

—the Tamhidat of Ayn al-Qudat Hamadhani

Master of the Jinn

For hours we waited, forlorn and silent as the circle closed. We could not sleep, and I was not certain that dawn would ever come again. The stars did not move as we sat together by the fire, wrapped in our frail blue cloaks against the unswerving storm of our destiny.

In truth, I had but half-believed that the whirlwind would ever come, fool that I am. Slowly, the distant, wailing sound reached our ears; at first like a high, shrill whistle that would not end, and then gradually increasing in strength and volume, as if it were gathering all other winds into its speed.

How vast must be this circle, I thought in awe and terror. There was still no sign of it, yet the great wind was sweeping ever closer, howling now as if the very breath of the heaven were descending upon us; the rending fury of the storm penetrated the very ear of the heart.

I could bear it no longer. I fell to my knees and lifted my face to the unmoving stars and cried out to God to deliver us. Over and over I cried, even unto Arcturus high overhead. May my soul be a ransom for that cry!

Rebecca knelt by my side and held me, but I did not cease from wailing until the *faqir* suddenly appeared out of the darkness.

"Untimely bird!" he shouted over the wind. "You crow before the dawn! Come now, we must do as we are bidden! It is time to depart!"

His voice froze my tongue, but Captain Simach jumped to his feet at the words. "Yes, yes! Now is the time!" he said, hurrying off to load the camel. His burst of eagerness ignited movement in the rest of us. Ali and Rami rushed to help him, while Rebecca and I put out the fire. The Professor tried to help the young Captain balance our gear and supplies on the humped back.

"What's the matter with you?" Professor Freeman shouted, unable to keep pace with his friend. Captain Simach had already unhobbled the camel and was leading him out of the *wadi*.

The *faqir* laughed. It was a deep-throated sound, sharp and hoarse. I had never heard it before. "O you who dwell in the prison of the four elements and five senses and six directions, we are led beyond the four and five and six. Do you not see? The spirit of the King has brushed his soul. It pulls him like a magnet and you must follow in his wake."

By a different path we marched out of the *wadi,* following hurriedly after Captain Simach in single file, guided only by the beam of his flashlight ahead of us in the darkness. I took the rear position, glancing only once over my shoulder at the abandoned Land Rover, our faithful chariot. We climbed slowly upward along the steep easterly slope of the *wadi*, following the natural contours of its formation: twisting now sideways, now back, then forward and up again. I could not have found this path in daylight, yet did not ask

how he knew of it in darkness.

The unerring sense that pulled him was now near its pole and we followed as best we could, often stumbling along the difficult way in our haste. Only the *faqir* moved along the narrow path with equal ease, as if he were long familiar with it, or could see in the dark. He had overtaken Captain Simach and the camel, and now led the way with surefooted certainty.

After an hour we were clear of the *wadi* and standing on the broad expanse of the *reg.* We paused only long enough to drink a sip of water.

"What about the caravan?" Rebecca asked, looking back down the trail "They'll be caught."

"They are in no danger," said the *faqir.* "The storm is not for them."

Not for them! Only for us!

And for hours more we moved swiftly in the dark with neither food nor rest, driven on by need and the thunder of the closing wind, until I felt the gravel plain turn to sand beneath my feet.

We had come at last to the true desert of the *erg*, and on the shore of that great sand sea we stopped beneath the shelter of a lone acacia tree as out of place as ourselves, rooted in the last bit of rocky earth left in the world.

I fell exhausted beneath its boughs, wanting only to sleep until the Last Day, but Ali and Rami lifted me to my feet. Captain Simach and the *faqir* were standing together facing eastward, still as carved stone. For an instant I dared hoped that they were greeting the blessed sun rising over the dunes, but it was no dawn that I saw coming hard upon us.

Over the rim of the world it roared with unimaginable speed, vis-

ible at last, a great whirling wall of wind from one end of the horizon to the other, black as the night and rising as it moved, until it covered the moon and obliterated the stars.

I could not see its limit; wherever I turned, it was. We were encircled, the narrowing eye within its whirling lid, and we could do nothing but wait for the lid to close.

The *faqir* did not move as the storm enveloped us, nor our brave Captain who stood beside him. Not even the terrified bleating of our camel stirred them from their guard. The poor beast was roaring and bellowing with his head down, maddened by the onslaught of the unearthly storm coming toward us in every direction. Finally, Rami tore the hood from his *gandura* and wrapped it securely over the animal's head and eyes, then struck his left foreleg until he knelt. Ali tethered him to the tree and Professor Freeman, Rebecca and I huddled with them, trembling between the great body of the beast and the tree.

A hundred thousand prayers our souls invoked as the storm came truly upon us. Captain Simach fell to his knees, transfixed, as the whirling black cloud of wind roared five thousand feet high around our frail lives; and still the *faqir* stood undaunted, rooted as the tree, lifting his arms to the wind as if in greeting and supplication.

"Play!" he shouted to Ali, his voice booming somehow even above the storm.

The word was caught by the wind and driven around us, echoing off its mountainous walls to our ears. Ali placed the *ney* to his lips with trembling fingers, the first notes awkward and fearful, but the reed itself seemed to calm his breath, and the *ney* of Ali became at that moment an instrument of the Unseen. Verily, it began to

weave its plaintive cry into the very fabric of the storm, the notes rising with the wind, echoing higher and higher, growing stronger, until its music filled the circle around us with a bewilderment beyond longing, as if the great vortex of the storm had itself become the *ney* and we were the notes it played. Slowly our bodies ceased their trembling, and slowly, slowly our hearts surrendered to its song.

And glory to God the Highest, for the eye did not close. The storm circled the tree and ourselves, and great bolts of lightening flashed high overhead, but it came no nearer; spinning like the wheel of heaven around the axis of our prayers, it obeyed the unseen boundary of its purpose.

What that purpose was I did not know, nor why we had been granted this respite from its terrible onslaught. Sandstorms in the Sahara have been known to cover thousands of kilometers, but this was not the desert storm that Captain Simach warned us against. No mortal being could have survived its rending fury; the driven sand of this mightiest of winds would have flayed the flesh from our bones and ground the bones into dust. Yet not a single leaf, not a hair, had been disturbed within the limit of its orbit.

Surrounded by darkness, like dregs in the cup, tears of awe and deliverance fell from our eyes. Ali was blinded by tears and could play no longer. The *ney* fell from his hands, and as one soul we prostrated ourselves to the Great Deliverer in thanksgiving for His Mercy. And we wept without respite, not daring to raise our heads until that same unforeseen sleep that had once overtaken our Captain overtook us, and closed our own eyes to the night.

Master of the Jinn

I asked, "Where is the rational soul to be found?"
He replied, "It is found in the subtle world."
—Nasir i Khosrow

How long I slept I do not know, nor when the dream of wind departed, but I remember the warmth of firelight on my face and awoke to soft, expectant voices murmuring nearby. I strained to hear their discourse, smiling inwardly when Rebecca asked someone if she should wake me.

"You cannot wake up a man pretending to be asleep," Captain Simach said, standing over me. I laughed and sat up.

"What's happened?" I asked, looking at the silvery mist of dust that colored the nightglow of the sky. The stars had not moved. The Gates of Heaven were still open.

"We've been waiting for you," he said.

"Why didn't anyone wake me?"

"Because we did not know what caused you to sleep."

I nodded, remembering the soft sleep that had overcome me like a blanket of refuge. My body felt refreshed and my consciousness alert, but it was no dream that I had awakened from.

"The storm . . .?"

Captain Simach glanced over his shoulder and stepped out of my line of vision. "The storm has revealed what was hidden!" he said.

And rising from the mist I beheld the ruins of a mighty city, half-buried beneath the sand; crumbling walls and archways and broken pillars stretching into the immense dunes now piled a thousand feet high around us. Only one structure remained intact, and that so near that our tree might have stood in its great courtyard; a strange,

circular building with a domed ceiling, like an ancient temple, or a tomb.

"What is this place?"

Professor Freeman shrugged, but I saw the excitement in his face. "I'm not certain. It is suggestive of . . . If I could only-"

"Not yet!" Rebecca said. "Not until we've eaten!"

There was no argument. And no cave. The faqir had been correct. We had been led by a different intention to a different purpose.

"Where is our guide?" I asked.

"Gone," Captain Simach said. He did not seem surprised. "But let us give thanks first, and then eat quickly and explore the ruins. Whatever is there, it has been revealed for our eyes."

To this we all agreed. The camel was unpacked and watered and left to graze. He was eager and hungry; apparently, he too had slept. Then, after prayer, Rebecca spread the *sufreh* and laid out a cold breakfast of bread and cheese and oranges. There was much to speak of, but we ate in silence, our glances straying often to the strange construct among the ruins. And I thanked again the Grace that had brought us thus far unscathed to complete the circle, if indeed this was its completion.

Captain Simach showed no disappointment that the storm had uncovered neither cave nor bones, but if his soul knew what we were led here to discover, his tongue did not speak of it.

The *faqir* had not returned, and we could wait no longer. Cup and plate were quickly cleaned and packed away, and we set out in anticipation toward the circular edifice, drawn like iron to its magnet. Every ruin contains a treasure, it is said, and there lay ours, if any we were meant to find.

The unmoving stars were unnaturally bright, allowing Professor

Freeman's trained eye to search the structure as we came near, pointing out the remains of pillars around the walkway that circled the building, and the remnants of an overhanging portico below the domed roof. He first walked around the building carefully, gauging its width and height, looking for clues to its age and use. We followed, as he instructed, in single file, stepping where he stepped so as not to accidentally disturb any artifact in the darkness. He was delighted to find that there were four high, open doorways facing the four directions of the compass, the westernmost in direct line with the tree. Light was also entering from above; either the roof had partially collapsed or it was built open to the sun and elements.

He was surprised, however, by the absence of visible markings of any kind on the exterior, neither glyph nor rune nor word in any language.

"That is extremely rare for either a temple or a tomb of this advanced architecture," he said, crossing the threshold of the eastern doorway.

His face sank in disappointment when Captain Simach's flashlight revealed only a round construction of black stone blocks. It was a meter high and perhaps three meters in diameter, and he thought at first that it might be an altar. It was positioned in the exact center of the structure, directly under the circular, open roof of the dome. There was nothing else inside but the sand-strewn polished stone of the floor.

No, there was something more. Even with bright starlight streaming in, the interior seemed darker and more foreboding than any tomb. A nameless fear gripped my heart, and the air felt thick and heavy in my lungs; as if some grim and terrible expectancy had cast its shadow across the millennia.

I began to repeat my *zekr*, walking forward slowly, silently, my apprehension increasing with every step, until we were all gathered at the black stones. A thick, round covering of solid wood was laid over it, cut to the exact size of its mouth.

"This is no altar," the Professor said, frowning. "Perhaps it's a well."

"Then I will not drink from it," Rami said.

The Professor nodded. "I doubt if there's any water left in it in any event. The wood appears to be cedar, though. It would weather without rotting." He bent to his knees and began to examine the stonework with a small magnifying glass. He went over each stone with the flashlight, moving first around the top layer and then slowly downward until he reached the bottom ring.

It took many moments, and in the long silence Ali and Rami began to shift nervously, their eyes scanning the dense shadows. They too sensed the dark longing in the *aether* around us. They moved closer to Captain Simach, who was standing beside the strange well and brushing away the sand from its wooden covering. Rebecca noticed their sudden movement and went to stand by her father as he worked on his knees. The faint scent of our fear became stronger as we moved closer to each other within that pervasive aura of expectation. Only the Professor seemed single-mindedly oblivious to its presence.

"These stones were not cut from black rock," he said, standing up after his examination of the bottom layer. "They've been blackened by fire. Very strange."

Rebecca asked if the rest of the ruins might be worth exploring, but Captain Simach would not leave the well.

"This is the place we've been drawn to, cave or not," he said. "The bones of the King may never again be discovered, but he has delivered his message. Whatever we're meant to find is here."

"Wherever *here* is," the Professor said. "There are no markings of any kind, not even a shred of pottery. What race could have built all this? The location fits into no known legend or mythology. It might as well be on another planet." He sighed and shook his head. "If only *Shayhk* Haadi were here. His knowledge of arcane religious symbolism is far greater than mine."

"I thought there were no symbols," Rebecca said.

"There are no markings, but even the architecture of a building is symbolic of its purpose, and the structure surrounding the well is certainly significant. I've never seen its like, but it was surely designed with some religious purpose. The open circle of the roof seems to be the same circumference as the well. I wonder if... "

He did not complete his thought, but began to walk around the perimeter of the structure, looking up at the vaulted ceiling. Twice he walked around the interior circle, absently rubbing a hand over his close-cropped hair. He then began to measure the diameter of the room, counting off, from the approximate center of the well, ninety-nine paces from east to west, and again from north to south. Rebecca followed closely behind him while I retreated to the eastern doorway and made notes by the light of the eerily bright stars.

After a few moments, Captain Simach called out to the Professor. He had cleared away the sand from the wooden cover and now focused the beam of his flashlight on a spot at its center.

"My God!" the Professor said, and I heard the sharp intake of his breath. "Come look at this!"

I began to repeat my *zekr* once more, both curious and fearful of

what had been discovered. Finally, berating myself as the poorest of choices to bear witness, I joined the others in looking over the Professor's shoulder. He had taken a soft cloth out of his pack and was dabbing it with some sort of cleaning solution from a small bottle. As Captain Simach held the flashlight, he rubbed it slowly over the weathered surface of the wood.

"See here!" he said, as the solution slowly dissolved the sandy grit. He placed his magnifying glass directly over the small indentation the Captain had uncovered. A six-pointed hexagram star came clearly into view, enclosed within two concentric circles.

The Seal of Solomon!

I heard Rebecca gasp, and my heart was racing. The center of the star was blackened and unreadable, as if the ineffable Name had not been meant for our eyes.

"It's as if it had been burned into the wood!" the Professor exclaimed, and cursed under his breath. "I don't understand it, but it *is* the seal. It must be! King Solomon has been here!" He looked up at Captain Simach. "But why use the seal ring to cover a well? What does it mean?"

The Captain did not answer. Handing me the flashlight, he placed the heel of each hand against the thick edge of the wood and began to push. The Professor and Rebecca immediately joined him, their backs arcing with the force of their exertions.

"What are you doing?" I exclaimed in horror. "Our guide has not returned, and you don't know what…"

But it was too late. The wooden wheel was anchored by no more than it's weight. In an instant it slid from the well. Ali and Rami hurried to help lift it off and set it on the marble floor.

We looked at each other and at the uncovered well. I had no

desire to look into the blackness, but could not help myself. I held the flashlight over the rim. There was no water visible.

"Why, the stone also appears blackened on the inside," the Professor said, looking at Captain Simach. The Captain nodded. There was only blackness as far as the beam could reach.

"The structure is open to the four points of the compass and also the fifth direction, up to the sky," the Professor said. "The well is the sixth direction, down. Why, it could almost be a three-dimensional representation of a hexagram. I wonder…"

Professor Freeman swung the pack off his shoulder and searched inside until he found his lighter. He then took off his *gandura* cloak and wrapped it around a piece of broken masonry, tied it into a tight ball and poured over it what remained of the solution in the bottle.

He glanced at each of us, but no one, to our everlasting regret, moved to stop him. He snapped the lighter and the balled cloak burst into flame. He threw it into the center of the well.

We peered over the rim and watched its light go down into the darkness; down, down beyond the depth of any well known to man, down until its fire was lost to our sight.

And still we peered into the blackness, expectant, waiting, held by the chilling awareness of its inexplicable depth; no human hands could have delved it.

"This is impossible!" The Professor shouted at last. The mocking echo of his words resounded within the fathomless pit, hollowing as they spiraled down until they too were lost.

Almost at once his words were answered by a faint, rippling wail. A brief flicker of flame appeared far below, as if the burning cloak had ignited some updraft at the limit of our vision. And it was rising.

The interior of the well was alive with fire, roaring upwards with impossible speed.

"Aayii!" Ali screamed, and in a heartbeat we were thrown backwards to the floor as a geyser of flame shot through the chamber and burst the stone circle above our heads.

I scrambled on hands and knees to the eastern threshold, choked with dust and fear, and beheld a column of fire soaring ever higher into the night sky. By my eyes, I swear the flames reached unto the very vault of heaven before it was turned away, and even then it extended two fiery wings nearly to the horizons before it fell once more, like the punishment of Sodom, on this nameless and forgotten city.

Down through the circle it came with an ear-piercing shriek, a raging bolt of fire that shattered roof and circle around us. I watched in frozen terror as the smokeless fire now roared above our heads, crackling horribly as it twisted and turned into hideous shape.

Captain Simach was the first to stand. He was covered with white dust and his face was streaked with it, but I saw him lift his head to the dark form and look fearlessly into the black and terrible face.

"Baalzeboul!" he said calmly.

The demon roared at the name, and the stones trembled to their foundation. My heart nearly stopped as he glared at the slight human figures below him.

Baalzeboul! Allah protect us! We have summoned the Lord of the Jinn!

But the demon's burning eyes barely noticed us. They looked only at Captain Simach.

"*Too late! Too late!*" roared the *Jinni*, and my heart nearly stopped as he reached out a fiery, claw-like hand toward the brave Captain.

Ali and Rami sprang forward and seized Captain Simach by the arms, throwing him backwards to the ground. I thought they were going to shield him with their bodies, but they began to move toward the demon.

"Stop!" I screamed at them, to no avail.

Even the demon seemed startled by their advance. I could not believe it. He began to descend back into the well.

After the burning form was lost from sight, they leaped to the top of the well as the fire descended after him. I will never forget the nightmarish vision; the two cousins looked at each other and clasped hands, then shouting *Allahu akbar,* they stepped into the flames and disappeared.

I staggered to my feet in shock, but my wobbly legs would not hold me and I fell to my knees. Rebecca's nose was bleeding and her hand was covered in blood, though she did not seem to notice it as she tried to revive her father. Blood ran down the side of his face from a gash on his forehead. Captain Simach was also slow in rising. He was holding the back of his head as if the fall had stunned him.

And still the well burned with unearthly fire, as if it were waiting for us also to enter. I felt as weak and helpless as I have ever been in my life. Tears streaked the stone dust on my cheeks as I cried out to God to help us. I was so overcome that I barely noticed the figure that ran by me.

The *faqir* had returned at last.

"Fools! What have you done?" he shouted, his eyes blazing with

anger as they searched the ruined structure. With a glance he absorbed the uncovered well and the wooden barrier on the floor, and who was gone and who remained.

"Fools, twice fools!" he said, hurrying toward the well. "Replace the seal!"

"Wait! What are-" I choked

"Silence!" he commanded, turning to me. His voice withered my question and his burning eyes froze my tongue. "Run! Run to the Master! Tell the tale! Only he can help them now!"

And he turned and leaped over the blackened stones into the flames.

Instantly, the fire blazed again, soaring through the broken circle into the sky. But the *faqir* did not fall. He floated in the flames, suspended and unharmed, like Abraham in the furnace of Nimrod, his eyes unwavering, burning like hot coals. I began to wonder if we were witnessing a miracle, but finally his hair and beard burst into flame, and his dry and wrinkled skin began to writhe, crack, and fall away; released from the spell that had knit its flesh, consumed at last by the dark and smokeless spirit of its origin.

Now the eyes burned with a pained, demonic fury as he towered over us, and the face contorted into the amorphous and horrible visage of his race, its monstrous maw filled with grotesque vampiric fangs.

"Ornias!" I gasped, the last word I was able to utter.

"The first of my names!" roared the *Jinni* as he sank into the flames. *"Did I not tell you I was the thief?"* Then he was gone, and the fire with him.

Ornias! Ornias! I repeated the name over and over without a sound. His last command as the *faqir* had closed my throat and cast

161

a spell over my tongue. Though I was stricken with grief and horror, I could think of nothing now but finding the Master. I barely had the strength to rouse the others, and could only gesture for them to follow me out of this accursed place. Captain Simach was peering into the blackness of the well with his flashlight and did not move, and Rebecca would not leave her injured father.

And so I ran into the night, my heart aching, my body and will compelled by the last human words of our guide, that diviner of hearts who was the thief of the wrong tale.

I ran through the ruins of the city and up the face of an enormous dune, sliding, falling, and finally tumbling over and down into the desert. And still I ran, until my lungs ached and I could run no longer, collapsing at last onto the sand, exhausted and alone beneath the unmoving stars.

The *Jinn*

O guide of my lost heart! Help me in the name of God.
For if the stranger is lost, only the guide can lead him.
—Hafez

Sunlight woke me, the heat pressing on my eyelids and startling my overburdened senses. I was shivering from the cold and it took me a moment to comprehend the truth. The blessed sun had risen at last. I raised my head from the sand to greet it, my soul rejoicing at the long passing of the night. Only when the chill had gone did I realize that I had fled without food or water, my legs commanded by a need stronger than sustenance or drink. I nearly laughed.

I had survived the greatest of winds and the mightiest of demons, and by the grace of *Allah* I would live to fulfill the task burned into my heart. The sun set my direction, and shunting grief aside I began to walk west and north across the *erg*.

For three days and three nights I walked before finally being reminded of my prayers by my insect brothers. Thus the Tuaregs came upon me and I was brought to Agadez. Here I have been well cared for, moving between delirium and the scribe's trust, silent but for my urgent pen, waiting for the Master's word.

A week has gone by, or two, or a month. I do not know. The two women who tend me will not tell, and no one else has come. They still whisper outside my door, but I no longer listen. My feverish pen has blackened the white paper. It is full written, stained with memory and tears. I have ceased from weeping and the inkwell is dry; the tale is told and my trust complete.

For days and nights more I slept, my frenzy spent beyond words. Always, I dreamt of the Master, until that morning when I found

him sitting beside me.

My lips formed his name silently, unsure if I was still dreaming, and I wept new tears as I kissed his hand. He greeted me with kind words that needed no answer, holding my right hand in both of his. The presence of the Master restored my spirit and his touch lightened my heart, as if he were absorbing the unspoken days and nights through my skin. I felt certain that he somehow knew all that had occurred, and again tried to form words, but he shook his head. "Do not try to speak," he said.

His voice was calm and reassuring as he placed one hand on my forehead and held my wrist with the other. I attempted to sit up, but he shook his head again and I fell back into the pillows.

He closed his eyes and mine closed as well, the subtle pressure of his hand on my forehead tugging at the veil over my memory. The journey rushed into my consciousness like a torrent and I trembled with buried memory: fear, doubt, amazement, despair and hope washed through me. And like the Great Physician who brings both pain and cure, he broke the spell over my heart.

"Now you may speak!" he said gently.

"Master," I whispered hoarsely, my throat muscles aching.

He gave me a sip of water and I sat up. In a croaking whisper, I told him of the storm and the lost city and the demon of the well. He nodded at the small table and the pages of my manuscript. "I have read your account."

"Master . . . The *faqir*, Jasus... He had other names, but they burned away in the fire. He... he is Ornias, the *Jinni* of the tale. I didn't . . ."

"He was not hidden from me," the Master said gently. "A worthy guide who led you well, as you have noted."

"But a *Jinni*! Like the demon Baalzeboul!"

"Alike, and yet not. You do not know his long tale, or the truth of his many names. Baalzeboul sensed him from afar and retreated, even as he reached out to the soul of the King in Aaron. Had you but waited for your guide to remove the seal, even the Lord of the *Jinn* would have been powerless before him. And he would have brought him glad tidings, for he was also a messenger."

A messenger? Glad tidings? I knew enough not to ask, though I did not know what else to say. That the Master had always known our guide's true identity amazed me beyond words.

The Master smiled at my contemplations. "You have learned how much you do not know, young scholar. The journey accomplished that much, at least."

At any other time, even this small acknowledgement would have filled my heart with joy, but I could feel little now except the burden of unanswered questions mingled with sorrow and loss.

"Master, poor Ali and Rami. They…"

"They did not fail in their guard, and blocked the portal with their human bodies, lest any other of the *Jinn* dared to come forth. They are held captive because of it and we must see to them now. Come, you are well enough. The scribe's work is not yet complete."

Ali and Rami held captive? Alive? My pulse quickened. *But in the land of the Jinn! God have mercy on them!*

I did not doubt that he knew. The *Qutb* is said to be the pole of both worlds, of men and *Jinn,* although I had always thought the latter no more than a useful metaphor. Indeed, the scribe's trust was far from over, and my heart rejoiced that they yet lived, even as it remembered the shame of having deserted the Professor and

my *darvish* brother and sister.

I asked after them, but the Master shook his head.

"Their long night has not yet ended. Only you were given safe passage to the dawn! But fear not, you will see your companions soon enough."

Safe passage? "Master, could not Ornias have saved us from opening the well? He can foretell the future."

"When the Gates of Heaven are open, there is neither past nor future, young scholar."

Of course! "Then what of-"

"Enough! Words will not satisfy your heart's inquiry. Tomorrow the desert will reveal the truth of the tale."

The desert again! I sighed, but actually felt little fear at the prospect. The Master was here, that most peerless of guides, and hope unlooked-for brought new energy and resolve to my limbs. Whatever doubts I once had were split like the scribe's reed pen, it's tip cut off even as the path of love severs the head of reason; and such a pen, cut from the reed-bed of the heart, says only *taslim,* "I gladly accept."

I dressed quickly and fell into step behind him, happy beyond words to be once more following in his wake. He led me to the courtyard of the *Amenukal's* home where we found the venerable old man sipping tea with Afarnou, his son. They stood as we entered.

"Welcome, twice welcome," said the *Amenukal,* smiling. "I am happy to see that you are well recovered."

I bowed to him and his son, thanking them as best I could for my succor, wiping away a tear for the companions I had left behind. Eloquence is dumbfounded by love, we say, and by grief also.

The *Amenukal* said nothing, but Afarnou looked sourly at me, like an unwelcome burden he was forced to carry. His father instructed him to bring tea and refreshments for the guests, and he glared at us before moving to obey.

"Forgive my son, " the old man said to me. "He is unaware of your journey, and does not understand your tears."

The Master nodded. "Tears were originally the blood of the heart. Grief turned them into water."

"Alas, it is so!" the *Amenukal* replied. "I fear he will learn it soon enough."

I looked from one to the other, not understanding the strange current of their speech, except that the *Amenukal* seemed to know something of our purpose. He was older than the Master, a man of influence and dignity all the more evident for his humility and noble bearing. Yet even he deferred to the Master, before whom all such qualities bow their heads in shame; and I sensed that the *Amenukal* was also a thread woven into the circle's tapestry.

After the evening meal, we sat once more in the courtyard as the *Amenukal* lit a fire in the stone hearth. Afarnou again brought tea, and I could hear the women talking softly in the kitchen. I had grown quite fond of them and their whispers in the weeks of my recovery, and they seemed delighted to have the Master among them. Afarnou's manner, however, was heavy with resentment.

"Do you really think the bone diggers are still alive?" he asked, shaking his head.

The question was addressed to his father, but the Master answered. "If it is God's will," he said. "Ishaq and I, at least, will leave at dawn to discover the truth."

"Their food and water would have been gone long ago. I warned

167

the fools that there were better places to search."

"No doubt you did, and for that may God lessen your account. But greed is a dragon. It cannot be hidden. You think it small and safe in your heart, but ever its head and limbs are bursting out."

Afarnou looked uneasy at the response. "Only a fool would chance the desert for old bones. Such useless nonsense."

"Even gold is useless to bones, my son," the *Amenukal* said. "And we shall all be bones in the end."

"Indeed," the Master added. "Better to seek after the good Goldsmith, whose work is wrought from true metal and is everlasting."

Afarnou had no appetite for such words. On the verge of anger, he stood and asked to be excused, then turned and walked quickly into the house.

His reaction saddened me. Neither his wise father nor the attention of the Master could penetrate his heart.

"His next journey will be his last," the Master said.

The *Amenukal* sighed. "As will mine," he said, rising and following his son into the house.

Their words made me frightened for Afarnou, though I did not know why. The Master put his hand on my shoulder.

"Do not sorrow on his account," he said. "God is not ignorant of any action. It is only His forbearance and mercy that prevents the evil action from being brought to light. Each man's fate is in the end the same, and Afarnou's heedlessness has written the moment of his own in this world. Alas, his camels are overburdened."

After a moment he also walked into the house, leaving me to put out the fire. I did not need to ask what he meant. *His camels are overburdened!* It was a common term, used to designate a smuggler. They had tried to warn him that he was in danger, but he had returned to the old Tuareg ways; pride and avarice had hardened his heart. I threw dirt on the fire, and as I watched the last glowing ember crackle and hiss out, I knew I would never see Afarnou again.

In the morning he was gone. Without a word he had taken his leave, spurred on by the dragon that bore him to his last caravan. Neither the Master nor the *Amenukal* spoke of it; they had seen his fate harden around him, and nothing could be done to sway it by even a hair's breadth.

Yet the day had dawned anew, and as we gathered for the morning meal my thoughts turned away from what could not be undone to what must be done. My brothers and sister would be desperate now, and I feared what they might dare out of hunger and thirst.

I did not speak of it though. We ate in silence, or rather, no word was spoken that my ear could hear. The Master and the *Amenukal* sat facing each other across the *sufreh,* and often they would glance at each other and nod or sigh, as if their thoughts moved to and fro beyond the need for speech.

Indeed, at meal's end, after the *Amenukal* had taken the dishes and *sufreh* into the house, the Master turned to me and said: "What you have learned, keep silent. And forgive our lack of courtesy. There was much to consider, and little time to do so. We must move quickly if we are to enter the circle before the fire dies completely."

The fire dies! They were the words King Solomon had spoken through Captain Simach. *But what fire was dying?*

He stood and I followed him through the courtyard gate into the

street. There waited the *Amenukal*, standing beside the very same Land Rover that had carried my companions and I into the desert. I could scarcely believe it. It had been washed and filled with supplies, but it was the same vehicle.

"Our host had it brought back from the *wadi*," the Master said. "As good a chariot as ever carried a king."

I beamed with delight as the Master entered the driver's seat and the *Amenukal* slipped in beside him. The engine roared to life as soon as I closed the back door and we drove through the narrow streets at breakneck speed. Even the desert did not slow us, the Master's certain touch guiding the vehicle as if it had taken on his will. We careened around boulders and swerved to avoid dangers I could not see.

All day we traveled, eating a little as we drove, pausing only for fuel and prayer. The desert sped by, changing from *reg* to *erg* at midday, from low, shifting dunes to ones hundreds of feet high. And still the Master drove relentlessly onward, finding valleys between the great sand hills and bringing us ever closer to our lost companions, waiting in the unchanging night.

At dusk we came at last to a barrier we could not cross. Encircling dunes, a thousand feet high and stretching for miles, blocked our way. He slowed to a stop. The Master had not once asked the way, and I marveled that without a word of direction from me he had driven unerringly to the circumference of the circle, the great sand mountains formed by that mightiest of storms. Over their rim was the nameless city that once lay buried beneath them.

The light was fading and we had little time left to reach the summit. The Land Rover was left behind as the Master led the way, the *Amenukal* right behind him, and neither weariness nor age seemed to deter them as we climbed the dune before us. The sand was amazingly solid beneath us, hard-packed and yet pliant enough to give way, almost as if it were forming itself into steps beneath the Master's feet.

The stars were already visible when we crested the dune and made our way into the valley of the lost city. At some point we must have again passed the Gates of Heaven, although I could not say where or when, for they had not moved above the ruins. I could see beneath their eerie brightness the ghostly white stone of the domed structure, standing broken and waiting above the rest.

We entered from the opposite end of my shameful flight, and were approaching from the west that single tree that had sheltered our company during the storm.

A fire was going, but I clapped my hand over my mouth when I saw three figures lying beneath the tree.

"Master!" I said. "We're too late!"

"Fires do not build themselves," the Master said softly. "And the dead have no need of them. Run ahead and wake them."

I ran swiftly over the rough stones, shouting as I approached, "Wake up! Wake up!"

My three companions jumped to their feet as I ran forward to embrace them. They were greatly relieved to see me.

"What happened to you?" Rebecca asked. "Where did you go?"

"I couldn't help it!" I blurted out, and told them in a jumble of words, my face burning with shame, about the *faqir's* last command, and how I was lost in the desert and rescued.

They looked at each other as if I had gone mad. "But you've only been missing for a few hours," the Professor said. "Didn't you hear us? We searched for you. We called your name."

I shook my head in astonishment, noticing the bandage on the Professor's forehead, and that Captain Simach's left arm was carried in a makeshift sling.

"But I've been gone nearly a month," I said. "And the Master has come back with me."

At that moment, the Master and the *Amenukal* stepped into the light of the fire, startling them.

"My God!" the Professor said. "My God!"

"Indeed!" the Master said, smiling. "Only by His will have you come thus far, even to the uttermost limit of the world."

Rebecca and Captain Simach stared at him in wonder, shaking their heads as if they had been awakened from a dream.

"Master..." they whispered together, and reached to kiss his hands. He embraced them both instead.

"Come," he said. "I have brought an old friend who knows something of healing. Let us rest by the fire and he will tend to your injuries."

The Master then introduced the *Amenukal*, who smiled and greeted them with courteous words, though briefly. The Tuareg are known for their taciturn nature. We sat by the fire, the Professor sitting down heavily beside me, never taking his eyes off the Master. His shoulders sagged, but it was more than weariness that afflicted him. I understood the burden of his disbelief.

Gently the *Amenukal* removed the Professor's bandage and examined the wound.

"A small cut," he said. "It has been well cleaned and will heal soon enough."

Rebecca nodded, thanking the old man when her father said nothing. Captain Simach's injury was also minor. The arm was

merely sprained, he said, and he had worn the sling only because Rebecca had insisted. He removed it now and turned his wrist to test its flexibility.

"Well enough," the Master said. "There is little time to rest if we are to deliver Ali and Rami safely."

This pronouncement startled them even more than his unexpected presence. The Captain and Rebecca were greatly relieved that our companions were still alive. They did not doubt the Master's word. Professor Freeman, however, still seemed to be in a mild state of shock. He had barely been able to accept that I had indeed been gone for nearly a month.

"But I saw them leap into the flames after that... that demon," he protested. "How could they possibly survive?"

The Master shrugged. "They were true to their duty and their love, and so the fire did not consume them. And the Lord of the *Jinn* will not harm them. They are not what he expected. My thoughts are even now with Ornias, and he is with them."

Professor Freeman looked at the Master for a long moment, and what he saw could no longer be denied. There were tears in his eyes.

"What a fool I've been," he said. "My mother's vision warned me to seek shelter, and I did not understand. *You* are my shelter, Master. I doubt it no longer. Will you not accept the most stubborn and foolish of your students as a *darvish*?"

"God is the only shelter, my friend," the Master said. "His wind was as the flood, and His mercy the ark that has brought you to safety. By His grace I welcome you."

Rebecca burst into tears and hugged her father, and I saw in her eyes the love she truly bore him, that she herself had come lately

and completely to accept. My heart also shared their joy. Even the shadows seem lightened somehow.

"Your initiation, however, must wait for now," the Master said. "The boundless universe may be finite, but the science of the heart is not. The immutable laws of physics hold little sway over the infinite planes of existence and the life that abounds there. Each instant the Beloved changes forms, and only His love and mercy binds the planets to their skies, to stand immobile, or turn in the heavens as they do now."

It took us a moment to comprehend the Master's words, and we looked at the sky in the same instant. It was true. The stars were changed. Sirius and Capella had already set. Antares and Vega were higher in the sky. The Master had come, and some unknown barrier had been passed. The stars that had been immovable in their stations were once again obeying their orbits. The Gates of Heaven were closing.

"Yes," the Master said. "Dawn approaches. It comes swiftly at the boundary of the world."

"Indeed," the *Amenukal* sighed, "already the guide of my people has set."

"Do you mean the star *Hugu* in the constellation Ophiuchus?" the Professor asked, pointing to the heavens. "I know it. Your caravans use it as a guide."

"*Hajuj,* we call that one," the old man said, looking into the fire.

I sensed that he was not speaking only of the star. The others did not know about Afarnou.

"The stars need no longer concern us," the Master said. "Though you have witnessed Baalzeboul unveiled, you do not know him. The heart of the *Jinn* is fire, and fire is his blood,

174

smokeless and everlasting, and he loves not man."

"Alas, it is so," the *Amenukal* said. "Older than the stars is the race of the *Jinn*, and great is the power that was native to them in their beginning. They cannot be harmed by mortal devising."

"Yet Ornias chose to cloak himself in the flesh of men," said Captain Simach.

"Yes, I wonder why?" the Professor mused.

"That you may ask him yourself," the Master said, "when you see him again."

Professor Freeman's eyes widened at the thought, but as usual my concerns were for my own safety.

"Would the *faqir's* touch have consumed us, then?" I asked, remembering the care he took not to come near us.

The Master shook his head. "The sense of touch is foreign to the *Jinn,* unless you also communicate on other levels. The gift of his humanity set him within human limits, but his innate nature was not changed. Even among his own race he was of a high station, or else the gift would not have been given. But that is another tale."

"Can he be trusted?" the Professor asked.

"I trust him."

There was no more to be said. The Professor nodded.

"When we cross their boundary, however, it is you who must keep your distance," the Master warned. "In their own land, their power could surely destroy you, if that was their intention. Beware most of all of Baalzeboul."

Beware indeed! I remembered vividly my own childhood and my mother's warnings about the terrible King of the *Jinn* who punished mischievous boys. I made a sour face and the Master laughed.

"You at least have nothing to fear, young Ishaq," the Master laughed. "No demon can withstand the speech of scholars." I laughed with the others at his jest, if jest it was. With the Master one can never be certain.

"Now be of stout heart, all of you," he said. "I assure you, God has not created in the earth nor in the heavens anything more occult than the spirit of Man."

We were heartened by his fearless words, and I did not doubt that he was, by God's will, the *Qutb* of all that lived under heaven, both men and *Jinn*, but my attention was caught by the first light of day appearing over the high dunes surrounding us. I had seen the sun of the world set barely an hour before, and yet dawn was already upon us.

"Swiftly now," the Master urged. "Light has not touched this land in three thousand years, and it will not linger." Without another word he rose and began to walk toward the structure that housed the well. We followed quickly behind him through the ruins.

In the short time it took to reach the well, the sun had already risen to the point of mid-morning, as if it were hurrying to reach its meridian and be gone from this dark longitude. The Master seemed unconcerned however, his brisk step as certain as the coming of the dawn. He entered through the great eastern archway and, without a glance at the structure surrounding it, went directly to the well and the wooden cover.

"Be careful!" Professor Freeman urged. "It is a deep well, like the gateway to *Janannam*, and can fill with fire in an instant."

"A gateway, indeed," the Master said. "You've remembered the lesson well, my old student. But that is only one form of the word." And he stood over the well and its wooden covering in silent

contemplation.

None dared to speak. *Jahannam* is the Muslim word for Hell, and whatever form it took, I could imagine nothing worse. The Master must have seen something else within his silence, however, for he gently touched the first two fingers of his right hand to his lips and placed them on the seal burned into the center.

The reverence of the gesture surprised me; and more, it somehow changed the *aether* around us. The sense of eerie watchfulness became at once greater and yet less menacing, as if our every movement and intention were perceived. If that was so, the Master did not hesitate.

"Remove the cover!" he commended, and the four of us quickly slid it free and set it carefully on the floor.

The *Amenukal* was the first to peer into the well and tears formed in his eyes. The black and bottomless void was now filled with the most perfectly clear water, still as a mirror and glowing in the refracted light. I could not believe it, reaching for its translucent surface as one lost in the desert reaches for a mirage.

"Do not touch the water!" the Master said, even as my hand began to move.

"What water is this?" the Professor whispered. "Where did it come from?"

"All torrents end in the Sea," the Master said, "wherefrom all bounty flows, even as all gifts are but a reflection of His bounty in this world. Had you waited for the *faqir* to remove the sealed covering, these waters would have greeted you then. The fire of Baalzeboul would have been stayed and Ornias need not have burned away his human form. Behold! Here is set a boundary that the *Jinn* dare not cross, the confluence of *Pishon, Gihon, Prath* and

Hiddekel."

"The four rivers of Paradise!" Professor Freeman exclaimed in astonishment.

The Master did not answer. He passed his hand across the perfect reflection and whispered an invocation I could not hear; and in that instant, as we peered intently into the water, the mirror became a window of what lay beyond:

Darkness unbearable filled the circle of our vision, and the circumference of the portal howled with an icy wind from beyond the void. A humming wind, greater even then the storm that had surrounded us in the desert: and it seemed alive, driven by desperation and a preternatural, pulsing rhythm.

Allah protect us! This was no mere vision, but the chilling and inevitable reflection of a moment long ordained, for there came into view an endless range of enormous black pinnacles higher than the moon. I could see them clearly in the still waters, rising vast and terrible beyond the rim of hope and light, burning since the beginning of time with the unending flames of despair.

The Mountains of Darkness!

I closed my eyes against the vision. I think I would have fainted had not the Master gripped my arm. I opened them again and the vision was gone. The others had also turned away from the hellish sight, but their eyes still held the horror of what they had witnessed.

I cannot do this! I thought, my heart beating wildly. Only the Master's firm hand on my arm kept me from falling to the floor.

Then came the light that ends all darkness, and chased the shadow from my heart. The blessed sun had risen directly overhead and a column of golden light streamed from its zenith through the broken circle of sky above us, as if it were seeking its own source in the untainted waters; and the water absorbed the light as it danced and sparkled on the surface like the polished mirror of the heart.

But now the level began to drop, as if the light were drinking it, or perhaps these purest of waters, void of anything but Love, would not be diminished and were retreating.

"Now!" the Master said to Captain Simach, and climbed nimbly to the edge of the well. The Captain instantly understood his intent and he helped the *Amenukal* onto the ledge. Rebecca immediately leaped up to join them, pulling her father after her.

I stood looking at them, torn between that vision of black despair and the pure reflection of Love that my soul remembered, until the Master gripped me by the neck of my cloak and pulled me up beside him as easily as if I were a child. The Master held my hand and also that of the *Amenukal*. I instinctively reached for Rebecca. She took my hand and her father's also, and he gripped that of Captain Simach. When the *Amenukal* clasped the Captain's outstretched hand, the circle was complete.

"Allahu Akbar!" the Master said. "Without God, the water of life is fire." And he stepped into the abyss.

Down he fell and we fell with him, the circle unbroken, bathed in the light of the sun. And the blackened stones of the well seemed to melt away from us as we moved down through the expanding shaft of light toward the retreating waters. My heart leaped to my throat as I looked down and realized that we were now falling free in space, caught like motes of dust in the light. The Master laughed as our robes whipped around us, and we plunged down and down and ever closer to the water, now glittering beneath us wide as the world, like six lost drops in this sea of illusion returning at last to the true Ocean. And that is all.

Master of the Jinn

The water of this ocean is fire;
waves come so that one would think they
were mountains of darkness.
—the *Diwan* of Hakim Sana'i

It is said that mysteries may be revealed to the spirit when the body sleeps, and that in dreams the soul remembers what it has always known.

Alas then, for I remembered nothing when the Master called me gently forth, his hand on my forehead, waking my floating awareness into consciousness from some great distance and a light brighter than Betelgeuse. For an instant, I thought I was back in the *khaniqah* and had overslept, but it was no earthly home that we had awoken to.

We were in an immense vaulted structure, beside a wide, burning pool of molten fire. The heat was unbearable and the harsh red light was painful to the eyes. The Master helped me to my feet and I saw an open circle of night sky high above us, utterly black and starless as the void.

"Master, where are we?" I asked, choked and trembling. My voice echoed wildly in the cavernous chamber.

"Where God has led us," he said softly, leading me slowly toward a great archway.

With each step away from the flames my strength increased, and his quiet assurance flowed through the hand on my arm, imbuing my will with courage. I was startled to find that my clothes were dry. I felt certain that we had come through water. *Had the heat dried them so quickly?* I could not remember. I glanced back at the

burning pool, and his last words before we leaped into the well resonated in my heart:

Without God, the water of life is fire!

I recoiled at the thought, and felt the Master's grip tighten on my arm. I repeated my *zekr* silently, wondering what would become of us. I knew we could not return the way we had come. We had leaped from light into darkness, and only by the grace of God could the Master guide us home again. He hurried his step and I gladly hurried mine.

The doorway was a great distance from the pool at the center of the chamber, and as we approached it I was overjoyed to find my companions waiting outside. I called out in greeting but they did not answer, and as we stopped beside them I knew why. We had entered into the midst of a dark and mighty city, and we stared in wonder and terror at what no human eye had ever beheld: The Land of the *Jinn*.

The towering Mountains of Darkness encircled us, looming as high as our sight could reach. Black as coal they were and yet eerily crystalline; and burning with a smokeless fire as spouting arcs of flame shot forth from a billion fissures to illuminate the starless night.

I felt lost in time, as if we had somehow emerged at the volcanic beginnings of the world; and indeed an icy wind howled without surcease, encircling all the land in unrelenting and bitter fury from some unknown source.

And my God, the vast city spread before us was stranger than anything I could have imagined. It seemed to be composed entirely of bizarre black pinnacles, many higher than earthly mountains, stretching across the plain in every direction.

Each seemed to be made from the same crystalline rock, a hundred thousand fires glowing in the enormous window-like openings cut into them, rising in convoluted spirals from the plain to the very summit. The strange design was broken only by hundreds of kilometer-wide terraces jutting into space at different elevations, each of a different geometric pattern extending from a great double archway. They formed an elusive symmetry that shifted when viewed from even a slightly different perspective. Walking half a step or the subtlest turn of the head dazzled the eye with unique kaleidoscopic visions.

"Do not stare at the terraces," the Master warned. "Their message is beyond your sight."

Message? Perhaps their geometry formed a language that could only be read from the air. I could discern no staircases, nor a single step to carry the weight of man. It was an architecture that defied all human limitations, inaccessible except to a race born with spirit wings.

Perhaps the spiraling buildings themselves formed some part of this language. They had been built in geometric clusters, reminding me somehow of the purposeful arrangement of our garden, though there was neither plant nor tree, nor growth of any color or kind.

Nothing will grow without God! I shuddered and looked at my companions. Only Professor Freeman's gaze had broken free of the strange and oddly magnificent city. He was looking behind us at the structure enclosing the burning pool.

It was of identical design to the one that housed the well among the desert ruins, though many times larger. What other impossible edifices were mirrored here in that long buried and forgotten city? The look of intense scrutiny on the Professor's face told me he had the same questions.

"Master, this place . . . What is it?" he asked numbly.

"The old tales name it *Jinnistan*," the Master said. "King Solomon himself is said to have commanded its building."

"Jinnistan!" he exclaimed. "And the ruins in the desert . . .?"

"Also built by the King. Once, their intentions sought each other, as darkness and fire seek light and water."

"What were their intentions, Master?" I asked.

"Knowledge and hope."

"What happened?" asked Rebecca.

"Knowledge destroyed one, and hope became despair. That is the true danger here," the Master said, sighing.

I swear that a billion fires seemed to burn brighter for an instant, as if momentarily fed on his compassion. "Yet God is the Most Merciful, and we have not come merely to search for baubles in the ruins of *Tadmor.*"

"Tadmor!" The Professor seemed truly shocked. "The ruins in the desert are *Tadmor?"*

"Yes," said the Master.

"Tadmor," he whispered, turning to Rebecca and Captain Simach. *"Tadmor* is the lost city that King Solomon is said to have built for the Queen of Sheba. The 'City of Magic' it was called, as she is sometimes named the 'Queen of Magic.' The old tales refer to it as a trysting place of spirits and demons, near the Mountains of Darkness."

"And so it is," Captain Simach said. He did not seem surprised.

"The grave of Sheba is also said to be there," the Professor continued. "The legend says that she was buried by Solomon himself."

Captain Simach said nothing. He looked at the *Amenukal*, who

stood next to him. They both had the same unreadable expressions.

"But where are the *Jinn?*" Rebecca asked.

The Master put a forefinger to his lips.

"Everywhere!" he whispered.

The word sent a shiver through me. There was nothing to be seen but the strange, enormously high pinnacles of the city and the even higher mountains, and endless fires illuminating a night of utter darkness. I strained to listen, but could hear only the wild, rhythmic beating of the wind.

"Well, what do we do now?" asked Professor Freeman. "Where do we go?"

The Master did not answer. He stood with his eyes closed, a sense of infinite kindness emanating from him, like a light in the darkness. And even as our eyes turned to him, he opened his, and his voice was gentle with reassurance.

"Wait now, and the way will be made clear," he said. "We are expected, and our guide has come."

We turned to look in the direction of his gaze and, walking toward us on a path that was not there a moment ago, came our guide of many names. Clothed once more in the guise of human flesh, he walked on a road of white marble flecked with gold. To our amazement, we too stood on the same road. It had materialized beneath our feet, and led from the vaulted structure behind us down into the city, curving out of sight between two slender towers of unimaginable height. Yet even the sudden appearance of the road could not distract me from the sight of Ornias, once more transformed as the *faqir.*

"Is he human again, Master?" I asked.

184

"No, the form he once inhabited has burned away and is no more. What you see is an illusion created for the sake of our human minds."

I nodded. The shadow-piercing eye of the Master could not be fooled, but I remembered the terror I had felt at the sight of his transformation. Was that the reason we have seen no other *Jinn?* Were they merely being considerate of our human sensibilities? I had no answer, but when Ornias came before us he prostrated himself before the Master.

"A thousand welcomes, O *Qutb* of men and *Jinn*," he said, his forehead touching the ground. "Hope returns to us at last. *Allah* is Most Merciful."

"*Alhamdulillah!*" said the Master. "All praise belongs to God alone, and indeed by His mercy we have come. Rise and be comforted, O *Imam,* most faithful of the noble race."

My companions and I stared in amazement as he rose to stand before us, once more our *faqir* guide of many names. The illusion was indeed perfect. He had been our most worthy guide, and although I had seen his true form, the hideous face and terrible fangs, the sincerity of his humility and obeisance to the Master shamed my fear. *Jinni* or not, he was a far better disciple than I.

'Now let us hasten," the Master said. "I would see my *darvishes* again."

"At once, O *Qutb*," said the *Jinni,* bowing low, and began to lead the way down the road. Ordinarily, no disciple would walk ahead of the Master, but I understood enough by now to know that he had been directed to do so without words. He had called him *Iman,* a designation not only of his steadfastness, but also of his high station; another of his names, and I thought we had learned them all.

The day was full of surprises, if day it was. As we walked in silence, I wondered if any sun had ever risen above these dark and fearsome peaks. And I saw no *Jinn*, although I imagined the eerie scrutiny of innumerable eyes. If they truly did not wish to frighten us, I for one was thankful of it. The thought of a thousand demons appearing all at once was unimaginable.

The Master looked at me out of the corner of his eye. "And do you also imagine that they do not know what you think of them?" he asked softly. "I assure you that your presence here is far more terrible to them than their appearance would be to you. Have a care!"

My face turned crimson at his tone, even though I did not fully comprehend the meaning of his words. All the tales I had ever heard of *Jinn* and *Ifrit*, of *Ghul* and *Si'lat*, had frightened me as a child, and he had read clearly the ignorance of my childish fears. The Master had named our guide *Jasus el-Qulub*, the Spy of Hearts, and though he had not yet acknowledged anyone but the Master, I repeated my *zekr* and asked silently for his forgiveness.

Nothing more was said. We turned to pass under the twin peaks and I beheld at last the end of our road and where it led.

In the center of the dark city there stood a human dwelling, a palace of crystal and white marble upheld by a multitude of columns, sparkling like a white jewel set in onyx.

"Behold, the palace of the King," said the *faqir*, sweeping his arm and bowing to us in a gesture of regal ceremony, like the King's chamberlain beckoning us forward.

Professor Freeman needed no urging; he could barely contain himself. Captain Simach stood looking at it with tight-lipped intensity, as if he were lost between remembrance and amazement.

Rebecca moved between them, holding each by the arm, waiting for the Master's word.

I did not know what to think. In the midst of a billion fires, the palace seemed to reflect only its own light, shimmering in the darkness like a mirage.

"Is it an illusion, Master?" I asked.

"No indeed!" he said. "Before you is the *Iahar-Halibanon*, the Forest of Lebanon, as it was called, the palace of King Solomon. A hundred cubits long, fifty broad, and thirty high it is, though there are no ceilings of cedar-wood, nor earthly wood of any kind. The *Jinn* built it at his command, and all their subtle skill went into its rebirth, though they could use only such materials as were found in their land. And therein is said to be the greatest of his treasures."

"The seal ring!" exclaimed Professor Freeman.

"We shall see," said the Master.

The palace was set high on its foundation, and on each of its four sides were broad stairs built for human feet. Thirty-three I counted as we walked up and onto a broad terrace, where we indeed found ourselves amid a veritable forest of columns.

Each seemed to be cut from a single crystal, its planes smoothed and polished to perfect roundness. And each glowed with a soft inner light. Here the Master halted, tilting his head as if he were listening to something. I strained my ears also, but could hear nothing, realizing after a moment that one of the things I could not hear was the wind. I stepped to the edge of the terrace and the howling assaulted my ears once more. When I stepped back, it was gone. *What is this strange power,* I wondered, *that holds at bay the fury of the wind?*

It was as if the circular columns were arrayed to form a barrier against the darkness of both night and soul, though I could not tell if the light emanating from them was some natural property of the crystal or wrought by the craft and skill of its artisans. I placed my hand on one and found it warm and tingling to the touch, a faint pulse beating within.

"Why, it's almost as if they were alive!" I said, but my companions had already stopped to marvel at them.

The Professor was greatly intrigued, examining one carefully under his magnifying glass. Captain Simach and Rebecca walked to another and each placed a hand on the same column. In that instant the light became brighter, and their two faces were reflected in the same glow. They looked at each other silently, an expression of surprise passing between them, as if they had never seen each other until that heartbeat.

The Master urged us forward, and as I stepped beside him my pulse quickened and my heart leapt for joy.

Praise be to God, I could hear the clear and plaintive sound of Ali's *ney!*

Its deep-throated cry was unmistakable, echoing down the halls of white marble and resonating against the columns until the palace was filled with its song. By some wondrous alchemy, the notes seemed to gather the soft candescence of the crystal and effuse both light and longing amid the pillars.

Our guide led us swiftly then to two great doors standing open before a magnificent chamber–the royal court of the King.

There was Ali at the far end of the room, sitting cross-legged on a low marble table. He was dressed as he was when last I saw him, and Rami sat next to him.

Alhamdulillah! I whispered, and my heart offered up a thousand prayers of thanksgiving. *Alive!* Even as the Master had said, they were unharmed and waiting.

On the threshold we stopped to listen. If they had heard us coming they gave no sign. Their eyes were closed, and Ali played as I have never heard him, each note as sweet and clear as sunlight on water. Then Rami began to sing:

> *The clouds of separation have been cleared away*
> *from the moon of love,*
> *And the light of morning has shone forth*
> *from the darkness of the Unseen.*

The timeless words held us transfixed, breathless, as the columns pulsed with the ancient song of absence and presence. Such was the state of *sama* brought on by light and song that almost I did not notice the one who sat and listened.

Across the length of the great room, on a high black throne he sat, though taller still was he, robed in black from neck to foot, and of a demeanor and bearing straight as any pharaoh bred to power. A high crown of deepest onyx, smooth and polished to mirrored luster, held fast his long dark mien, which framed like a cowl the most fearsome visage I ever wish to see. His grim features were as sharp and hard as if cut from stone, and his eyes burned like the mountains.

I knew that this was also an illusion, a spell cast for the benefit of his captives and now the new arrivals to his kingdom. But I remembered the terror of his first coming, roaring out of the well like a pillar of fire to the very limit of the sky. Black as pitch was

his face then, and I wondered if he chose this form to cower them into submission, or if some innate law of symmetry governed even this power of the *Jinn*–that the outward form must match the inner state. Thus Ornias could appear as our *faqir* guide, and surely this was the other: Baalzeboul. Lord of the *Jinn*.

Even now I would have quailed in fear had he turned his gaze on me alone, so stern and terrible did his countenance appear; but if he sensed our presence he gave no sign. He cast one great hand over his eyes, perhaps in contemplation of the song.

Only for a moment did the Master allow the song to continue, and then clapped his hands once. The sound echoed like thunder among the pillars and instantly they were aware of us.

Baalzeboul raised his head slowly at the intrusion, turning his imperious gaze upon us without concern, as if our presence were long expected. Ali and Rami were startled out of their reverie, however, ending the *sama* with a shout of delight.

"Master!" they exclaimed together, and the lights of the pillars seemed to pulse the brighter with their joy. They ran and prostrated themselves before the Master, but he commanded them to rise and embraced them together.

The *Jinn* Lord had not stirred through all this, nor changed expression. He regarded us silently, and I could not tell if his gaze was one of resignation or disdain.

"Will you not also greet the *Qutb*, O King?" asked Ornias. "He and his companions have come through fire and deep water at our need."

Baalzeboul stood to the full height his human-like form would allow. But he looked only at the Master, and his eyes seemed to pierce the very air.

"I am aware of all that passes through this guarded realm, " he said, his voice low and harsh as rushing flame. "By God's command were the boundaries set, and by His will alone you could have passed. But to what purpose have you come? Your servants are returned to you, yet your mind and thought is hidden from me, as man is ever hidden beneath his tongue. Speak! What song have you come to sing, O *Qutb* of men and *Jinn*?"

The discourteous words angered me even through my dread, but the Master met his eyes without fear.

"By His command indeed are the boundaries set, and by His wrath, as you well know. Yet, if you do not know my mind, I know yours."

And of all wonders, the Master did indeed begin to sing:

> *The meadow of my thought grows naught save grief,*
> *My garden bears no flower save that of woe;*
> *So arid is the desert of my heart,*
> *Not even the herbage of despair grows there.*

These words of separation and loss were as ancient as Ali's song of hope; and the lights of the columns grew dim as he sang, casting our long shadows in semi-darkness, though the *faqir* and the King cast none.

The Jinn cast no shadow!

What the Master's intentions were, I could not guess. As his deep basso voice echoed in the fading light, the King's eyes blazed like wheels of fire. I thought we were doomed.

As the last echo died into silence, I expected bolts of flame to spring from his eyes and consume us, but the Lord of the *Jinn*

seemed to buckle under the weight of the Master's song. Slowly, he fell to his knees, as if the words were a burden he could no longer bear.

Even thus he was nearly as tall as a man, though his eyes had dimmed to points of amber flame. The song had struck him to the heart and he could not speak.

Baalzeboul struggled to rise, but the Master raised his hand and the columns flared immediately into brightness, like unto the full light of day. The King cast an arm across his face and remained on his knees.

"Fear not," the Master said softly, " for I bring thee glad tidings. The spirit of Solomon, the great King, has sent the message of thy need across the ages, and his soul has interceded for thy kindred before the True Throne."

I heard then a rush of sudden moaning, like a brisk and fleeting wind. The *Jinn* who were everywhere had heard the Master's words. Baalzeboul lowered his proud eyes and all disdain vanished. He bent slowly forward until his dark brow and the high crown upon it touched the white marble of the floor.

"Indeed, the fruit of repentance is ripe when the branch hangs low," the Master said. "Rise now and take heart, for I bring thee the hope of God's mercy."

Baalzeboul raised his head, but did not stand; and even on his knees there was power and great majesty in his bearing, as evident in him as it was hidden in the *faqir*. He raised two great hands in supplication.

"O Master of *Jinn* and men," he said, "a thousand blessings on thy words. Since the beginning of the world our heedlessness has made us outcast, and only as slaves of Solomon the King did even

hope abide. But too long has his spirit been departed. The poison of the *Ifrits* has spread like a plague of rain, and the fire is nearly extinguished."

I was strangely touched by the anguish in his words. The spirit of King Solomon that had spoken through Captain Simach had indeed said, *"The fire dies!"* But if hope was the fire, what hope had he been, and what mercy have we brought that would keep it alive?

"*Alhamdulillah!*" the Master said. "Verily, both *Jinn* and men must reconcile themselves to God, or else suffer darkness and affliction. But I have brought both the messenger and the message. We shall speak to the Assembly together." And he called the *Amenukal* and Captain Simach to stand beside him.

Baalzaboul rose to his full height then and looked down at them keenly.

"They already gather," he said.

Thus the moment had come when all our labors would bear fruit and the circle close. The Master turned to us and commanded that we remain here in the company of Ornias. "He will guard you against any mischief while we are gone." And with a swirl of robes he turned and walked out another great door at the far end of the court, the *Amenukal* and Captain Simach behind him. And lastly walked Baalzeboul, the dark Lord of the *Jinn*.

I looked at my companions. Ali and Rami seemed content to wait as they were bidden, sitting in contemplation on the cold marble floor, but the Professor and Rebecca appeared as anxious as I at the abrupt departure of the Master. I hurried to the door, the Professor and Rebecca right behind me. Ornias said no word to

hinder us. None was needed.

Only a moment had gone by before we were out on the terrace at the rear of the palace. At once, the howl of the wind pierced our ears, but we were more amazed to see that the Master and his company were already down the steps and far into a dark valley, their way illuminated by the innumerable fires burning on the mountains.

That they had already gotten so far made it clear that we were not to follow them. The Master's command obeyed itself.

We watched until we could no longer see them. When we returned to the throne room in silence, the *faqir* was waiting.

"You need not fear for them, or for yourselves," he said, looking at me. "The *Ifrit* cannot harm them, and their malice cannot enter here. And your Captain is safe with them," he added, looking this time at Rebecca, who acknowledged his words with a shy, blushing nod.

The *faqir* sat cross-legged on the low table that Ali and Rami had occupied. We sat at his feet. There were no cushions or comforts, neither food nor water, but he bade us eat and drink what we had brought with us in our packs.

We ate a little and drank in silence, glancing at each other. The Professor bit his lip in consternation. The *faqir*—I cannot help thinking of him by that name—smiled kindly at us.

"The Master knows your minds also," he said, "and has commanded that I answer your questions as I may. Ask what you will."

"What is happening?" Professor Freeman asked, somewhat relieved.

"They are going to the Great Assembly of the *Jinn*, so that all the noble race may hear the message and see the messenger."

"And Aaron, Captain Simach, is the messenger?" Rebecca asked, now looking even more displeased at being left behind. The *faqir* nodded.

"But what is his message? What does it really mean?" Rebecca asked.

"Did you not understand the Master's words? He has brought us the mercy of hope."

"Hope of what?"

"Awareness of God."

Rebecca stared at him in astonishment, but I remembered what he had said aboard ship, that even the inhabitants of Hell are happier than they were in the world, for they had awareness of God.

"When was it lost?" the Professor asked.

"At the beginning of the world."

"How?"

"By failing in our labor of obedience to Him. Thus we committed the greatest sin of those who know the Truth, both men and *Jinn*."

"What sin?"

"Ingratitude."

> *I have not created Jinn and men*
> *except that they might worship Me.*
> —Koran LI: 56

Ingratitude!

I knew what he meant: the word he had used was *kofran*, whose literal meaning is to hide or deny. Ornias had evoked the inner meaning, as a Sufi would, to express the ingratitude of concealing God's bounty by denial, by rejection of Him.

Ali and Rami also understood, though they had no need to comment. The brave cousins had obeyed the Master without question, going into the fire willingly to protect their charge. Only Rebecca and her father were uncertain.

"I'm not sure I understand," said Rebecca.

"Nor I," admitted Professor Freeman.

"To understand the cause of our despair, you must know our tale from its beginning," said Ornias. "To know our hope, you must understand Solomon the King. Once I dared to steal the ring that made us his slaves, taking his form and his place on the throne, but I was confounded by his wisdom and mercy. In the end it was I who took his place in the tomb so that he might journey to meet his true fate. Solomon was my first Master, and at the last, my friend."

"The tale of that theft is written in the ancient lore," the Professor said.

"It is said that he had power over the wind," added Rami.

"And that he knew the language of the birds," said Ali thoughtfully.

The birds! I had forgotten the birds!

"Will you not tell us the full tale?" I begged him.

"Yes, tell us the truth of it," Professor Freeman pleaded, "and of his seal ring, if you will, that our hearts may also be certain."

"Ah, but I have no human heart to convince you of its certainty," said the *Jinni*, and there was almost affection in his voice.

"What do you mean?"

The old *faqir* sighed, and for an instant I could see the preternatural fire behind the illusion of his eyes; it made them seem as ageless as the stars.

"I mean that the piece of flesh called the heart exists in madmen and saints and children alike. It is only flesh, not intellect, nor spirit, nor knowledge, though humans often refer to it as such. Yet each atom, each cell of your body already knows the truth without understanding, as does this spirit of fire that is mine. The truth is apprehended by *life*, not by reason, and that is the heart of it. But all tales must wait for now. The Great Assembly is already gathered, and the Lord Baalzeboul stands before them."

"How do you know?" asked Rebecca, her voice edged with concern.

"The *Jinn* are mirrors of each others thoughts, and our awareness is beyond the limits of the five senses and the six directions. We need no human eyes to see, nor tongue to tell the tale."

"That's well and good for you," Professor Freeman said. "But we are not so fortunate. Why couldn't we go and see this assembly for ourselves?"

"You were not invited," said Ornias with a smile. "But the Master anticipated your desire. I will be your guide still, and your eyes if you will allow it."

"How?" asked the Professor.

"The web of our senses are not human, O sage, but since the birth of man and the fall of *Jinn* and Angels, we are compelled to mortal form in the presence of humans. Yea, even unto the degree of our ingratitude, fair or foul. I will guide your human senses and you will see a reflection of what I see, and hear all that I hear. Close your eyes, all of you, and remain silent. I must shield you from my brethren, for their minds together would overwhelm you."

The Professor and Rebecca willingly assented to attempt it. Ali and Rami also seemed excited by the strange prospect, and I did not doubt the *faqir's* words, or his power. I set pen and paper aside, and we closed our eyes together.

The lights of the columns had returned to their normal brightness, casting a faint red glow on our eyelids; and we gasped in shock as the *Jinni's* mind enveloped ours, and again in amazement as the red glow dissolved slowly into a clear and telepathic vision.

Praise God, I did *see* the Master, and Baalzeboul and the *Amenukal*. Captain Simach was behind them also, unmoving, his head lowered. They were all standing on a wide outcropping of rock overlooking a vast, deep valley surrounded by mountains. The land was ablaze with living fire, and even as we watched a shower of flames arced across the night sky like shooting stars, blazing to earth until the entire valley was filled. The mountains too seemed to be on fire as the remaining *Jinn* filled their slopes; and within the moving flames I glimpsed many a dark countenance, grotesque and horrible to look upon. Legion, they seemed, though some were fairer and held their place with grim dignity; and scattered among them were female shapes also, and *Jinn* of seemingly different ages—the younger ones smaller and golden flamed, flecked with red, and the elders, old as the world, burning nearly white with the amorphous fire that is their natural state. How they swirled and shifted around us, the entire race of the *Jinn* uncloaked, silent and waiting.

By shifting his awareness among them, Ornias allowed us to view the scene from different perspectives. At first we were far away at the end of the valley and the Master appeared small and distant. Then we were closer, at the foot of a mountain, then high above them on another. The swift changes were slightly dizzying until we settled very close, to their left and a little below. I saw Baalzeboul raise his hands, his black crown glittering red in the reflected light of his people, and he spoke with a human voice, or so it seemed to me, and cried out over the valley:

"Hear now, O *Jinn*, my brethren, *Jann* and *Ifrit* and *Ghul*, and rejoice! For the spirit of the great King has ascended at last to the First Realm, and his oath he has kept. His soul has interceded with the First Flame, and by His Mercy the messenger has come with hope renewed."

"The messenger, the messenger . . ." I heard countless minds whisper in unison, over and over and over, until the words become a chant and the strength of their desire nearly stopped my breath. The Master then eased Captain Simach gently forward so that he stood beside Baalzeboul at the edge of the rock; and he who had kept his face lowered raised it now, so that the fires shown clearly on his human features.

"Beniahhhhh!" they shouted with one voice, and we were utterly amazed. They had named him King Solomon's champion, one who they remembered; and their cry was of a great multitude. Now the quiet young Captain we had known raised his right hand as if he were truly the King's own herald, and spoke clearly in human voice.

"My first Master is departed forever, and the King whom all here served now serves the One," he said. "But I have been given to carry his message across the ages to another, greater than kings!" He bowed his head again and there was not a sound in the land of the *Jinn*. Even the wind had slowed to listen. When he raised his head once more, his eyes were alive with a light not reflected from any fire, and in his voice was a strength I had never heard in him. It carried above the wind and across the valley to the mountains.

"This is he whose footprint is known to the valley of Love. He whom the Temple knows, and the unhallowed territory and the holy ground. This is the son of the best of all the servants of God, the pure, the eminent, the elect. Hear, O ye who believe, for the *Qutb* has come."

I held my breath as he lowered his eyes and stepped back. And the Master came forth, even to the very edge of the rock. Still there was no sound, and a billion souls waited for his word. His eyes were kind and noble, patient and without fear. A light was in his face and his white robes shown like snow in the moonlight. He raised his eyes above the valley and the mountains to the Void, and his deep voice filled the night.

"Allahu akbar!" he said.

"Allahu akbar!" a billion minds replied, and even shielded by Ornias I was shaken to the soul by the power of their great longing.

And then the Master turned his back to them and, raising his hands to his ears, he said again, *"Allahu akbar!"* and began to recite the prayer. As he completed the first *rak'at*, the entire valley of the *Jinn* bowed their fiery brows to the black ground, and rose and prostrated again, the sea of fire moving like waves as they followed the Master, who led them as their *Imam*.

200

Allahu akbar! The mountains shook and the city trembled, and the prayer of the *Jinn* went out even unto the Void.

I cannot begin to describe the sincerity of emotion I felt from them, and wondered how long it had been since last they prayed.

"Not since the birth of man, young scholar," I heard Ornias reply in my mind, "has an *Imam* come who has given us a hope of answer."

And so it was that when the final prostration was completed, the Master, still on his knees, raised his arms to the darkness beyond the mountains in silent supplication, and after an endless moment he rose and turned again to the valley, and an immense weight of expectancy reached out from a billion ancient minds.

The Master lifted his hands over the multitude, and his deep voice boomed forth:

"*O believers, repent unto God with a sincere repentance!*" he said, and the words of the Koran echoed from the mountains. "Thus is it written, for repentance is the first station of pilgrims on the way to the Truth, as purification is the first step of those who desire to serve God."

Moans and great wailing greeted his words, and the wind began to howl more furiously than ever. Even the will of Ornias could not shield us entirely from the myriad and alien thoughts that came cascading into our awareness; the barrage at first was nearly overwhelming, but the mind of our guide quickly filtered them to a level of human endurance and understanding. Many had felt the light of hope rekindled, but others were plagued with impatience and doubt, and many more were filled with anger and disbelief, shattering the silence.

From the mountains and the valley those thousands of the *Jinn*

who did not heed the call and were longest in evil service began to rise and soar away, ascending like comets into the night.

One of the last of these rose to a great height, towering above the ledge and the Master, and he bore the gruesome countenance of an *Ifrit* filled with bitter malice.

"Fools!" he shouted, his voice roaring over them like a curse. "Free were we created and free did we live, before the plague of man. The son of David made slaves of the noble race, and never will I bend my spirit to another human Master."

"Then begone, O ignoble one!" commanded Baalzeboul. "You scorn what is beyond thy understanding, a gift that is freely given, and cloud thy spirit of thy own free will. Thus did God's wrath bind us. *Iblis* is thy true master, first in pride, and first to raise the stench of doubting smoke that blinds the mercy of God. Go then! And thy accursed kindred with thee!"

The *Ifrit* flamed still higher at the insult, while others of his kind rose about him in support. But the Lord of the *Jinn* did not falter, glaring at them silently from his tiny human form until even I felt the struggle of their wills in my mind, for it was there they fought and there their power lay. Other minds joined them, the hideous *Ghul* to the *Ifrit* and the *Jann* to the King, shifting the balances of power. Blasting curses were hurled like weapons, and spells were cast and countered, and almost I opened my eyes to escape the fury of the battle. But many more among them were uncertain and did not move to either will, awaiting the outcome.

Praise God that it was over quickly and did not come to worse, though it may have lasted for centuries in this timeless realm for all I know. At last, Ifrit and *Ghul* gave way before the greater strength of Baalzeboul's elder knowledge and the mightier fire of his will,

and they too sped away. Still I was shaken, even shielded as I was, by the power hidden behind the illusion.

The Master had not moved through all this, nor sought to weigh the outcome in any way I could discern, but now, though the wind roared like a tempest, the Master's voice boomed above it.

"Hear ye, O sons of the Most High. I have not come beyond the set boundary except by His will, and for His mercy. God has forgiven the son of David for his heedlessness, and his seed He no longer afflicts. Will He then not also forgive thee? Yea, for I am come with the fruit of His mercy!" And he beckoned to the *Amenukal*, who stepped beside him. I had almost forgotten the old man in the swift turmoil of events, but the *Jinn* that had remained seemed to know him without introduction.

"Naqib!" they whispered to my mind.

Naqib! Now I knew him also.

Here at last he was unveiled as one of the *awliya*, the friends of God, even as it is written in the Koran, *"Verily, on the friends of God no fear shall come, and they shall not grieve."*

The *Jinn* had known it immediately as he stood before them, and now we saw him revealed, his face luminous with the light that casts no shadow.

The fruit of His mercy, I thought, and with the sudden quickening of truth I knew that this was the real thief of the Master's tale, who had been cleansed by the blessed waters of forgiveness.

Did Ornias know this also? I wondered.

"One thief knows another," came his answer to my mind.

I did not know if Rebecca or her father understood, but it is one of our traditions that God has friends whom He has especially distinguished by His friendship and has favored to manifest His

actions, in order that the signs of the Truth may continue to be clearly seen through their spiritual influence. Among them are four thousand who are concealed and do not know one another and are not aware of the excellence of their state, but are hidden from themselves and from mankind. But others there are who know one another, and who have the power to loose and to bind; three hundred called *Akhyar*, and forty called *Abdal*, and seven called *Abrar*, and four called *Awtad*, and three called *Nuqaba*, (whose singular is *Naqib*) and one called *Qutb*.

Thus my Master, who is the *Qutb*, called forth for all to hear: "Here is come one whom by God's will is chosen as thy hope of Him, for King Solomon's last prayer was answered, and God the Most Merciful has raised up for thee a second hope, even as thou once scorned the first!"

And the *Amenukal* bowed low to the *Jinn*, in utmost humility, and though he spoke in the softest of voices, all perceived his words.

"Peace be unto you, who have been steadfast only in despair! My tale you know. By my own will I rode the steed of heedlessness, until I had become the lowest of the low. And when my despair was greatest, and I had lost all hope, God raised me up, even to the throne of His compassion."

Sighs and great moaning greeted his words, and my mind tingled with the thread of hope in them. I could feel the current of it even in the *Jinn*.

The *Naqib* raised both hands and closed his eyes, and soundlessly his thought and the weight of his attention went out to them, from mind to endless mind.

"Verily, though I am less than the dust beneath His feet, for thy

204

sake, thou who long for Him still, I am come by His mercy to dwell among thee, as thy servant and guide. Now the long path lies before thee. Come ye now all who will!"

At this Ornias abruptly broke our connection. Sudden blackness came over us until we blinked our eyes rapidly open. My head ached with the swiftness of it, so absorbed were we in the drama that had unfolded before our mind's eye.

"What happened?" asked Professor Freeman.

"What you were meant to see, you have seen," said the *Jinni*, "The last Great Assembly of the Noble Race. There will not be another."

"What will the *Ifrit* do now?" I asked. The evil I had felt in their onslaught made me shudder.

Ornias was loath to answer, choosing his words carefully, as if they were painful to him. "Their path is hidden from me," he said slowly. "Of my own kind, I have no foreknowledge, though I do not blame you for your response. You have not known them as I have. First they were of the noble race in praise of Him, behind *Azazal* alone, before he was cast down as *Iblis,* the great Satan. Alas, they are no more evil than any who are so veiled from the Light. Hope is slow to rekindle in them, yet their malice was like my own before Solomon bound our mischief to his will. What is a blessing to one may be a curse to another. They hate him for it still and grow ever more hideous within the grip of that hatred, and the envy and pride which are its brothers. For now they have retreated before the greater will and spellcraft of Baalzeboul. Yet by God's mercy, the Way has been made open to them also, though I fear they may be long in coming to it."

"So it is for the *Jinn* and men alike," said a deep voice behind me.

The Master had returned, and Captain Simach was with him. They had returned as swiftly as they had departed, and though the *Naqib* and Baalzeboul were not with them, we were overjoyed to see them both safe. He sat down next to me and Rebecca shifted over to make room for the young Captain. Professor Freeman now turned his attention to the Master.

"But the *Ifrit* also joined in the prayer," he said.

The Master did not answer, exchanging glances with the old *faqir.* A look of sadness came over the human features of Ornias, but it was the *Jinni* within him who spoke. "Humans may worship God by word and deed, yet rarely do so, while we who would, cannot. Alas, we were cast out from the joy of Him. We are barren. But the depths of our souls remember still the splendor of the sun that does not set!"

His voice was filled with the pain and longing of his race, and it touched my heart, yet there was acceptance in him also, a quality akin to the contentment of one long on the path.

The Master nodded, looking at each of us in turn. "All souls remember the sun that fails not," he said. "And by God's will, the way has now been made open to them also, to choose His mercy as once they did His wrath. Many an *Ifrit* may turn aside from it, and many another will be long in coming to it, but even now some of them have returned, and the *Naqib* leads them as *Imam*, with King Baalzeboul beside him. By their ingratitude the second children have fallen lower than the third, but all *Jinn* know well, as men do not, how it will be when God calls them to Judgement.

"Even now they call out *Allahu akbar*, whose real meaning is, 'We have become a sacrifice before Thee, O God!' And they are drawn up in ranks to perform the prayer, as both men and *Jinn* will

206

be before Him on the Day of Judgement. For on that day God will ask them both: 'What have you produced for Me during this term of respite which I have given thee? In what work have you brought your life to its end? Speak plainly! How have you dissipated the senses I have given thee? You have expended eyes and ears and intellect, but what have you done with them? I gave thee all of these to till the soil of good works, now display to Me your harvest! I gave thee bounty, now where was thy gratitude?'

"And then all men and *Jinn* must lift up their heads and answer, and then will great wailing be heard, and tears of contrition that were never shed in life will flow like a river. Alas, when the ship is sinking, all are sincere in devotion to God! Yet He is the First and Last and Ultimate, merciful and benevolent. Verily, His Love and Justice and Wrath and Mercy are One, and not forever will He afflict any of His children. God best knoweth the right course."

The Master's words cut out our tongues. I had never heard him speak so, yet knew that the *Jinn* who were everywhere heard all that was said.

The Master's eyes caught mine as if he read my thought. "Write this also, young scholar," he said. "Man and *Jinn* have no part in repentance, because repentance is from God to His creatures, not from them to God. It is a Divine gift, and may all here be worthy of it, for it is given when He wills, and to whom He wills, as the two thieves in our company will bear witness."

"I am become content with whatever He wills," said Ornias. "As was Solomon, who's wisdom returned at the last, for he repented of his heedlessness and ingratitude before his end. Now the circle is

207

complete. The messenger has returned as he was bidden, and the way has been made open for hope."

"Forgive me, Master," I said, "But what 'way' has been made open?"

"If your eyes and ears have been closed, open them now," the Master said. "By the mercy of God, this second palace of King Solomon has become the *khaniqah* of *Jinnistan*, with the *Naqib* as its Shaykh. Now let all *Jinn* come who will, for their hope of God is here."

I gasped in surprise. My eyes and ears *had* been closed.

"Close your mouth also, O scribe," the Master laughed, "and write that to worship God is to serve *all* His creation, and that the Path of Love is now the hope of men and *Jinn* alike.

The sincerity of the Master's words warmed our souls, and his attention, stern and yet filled with loving kindness, affected our hearts in a manner impossible to describe. Even the lights of the columns seemed to burn more brightly with longing, which is surely the beginning of hope, as love is it's reality. I sat silently and repeated my *zekr,* and the Sacred Tradition came into my heart and sat with me: *"I am close to the thought that my servant has of Me, and I am with him whenever he remembers Me. If he remembers Me in himself, I remember him in Myself, and if he remembers Me in a gathering, I remember him better than those in the gathering do..."*

Professor Freeman, not yet a *darvish*, was moved nearly to tears, and Rebecca glanced at Captain Simach with a look I envied.

"Aaron?" she asked after a moment. "They called you Benaiah. How is this possible?"

"I think we're related," he said with a smile.

"Indeed!" said Ornias. " His blood runs true. The *Jinn* can see it, even if you cannot. The circle of this destiny links many lives."

"I think I understand a little," said Professor Freeman. "Its in the First Book of Kings. Because Solomon had turned his heart away from God, all the kingdom except one tribe was promised to Jeroboam after his death." He opened the small bible he carried in his pack and read: "*'And I will for this afflict the seed of David, but not forever.'*"

Not forever! It was the cry of the King through the flesh of Captain Simach, and had finally come to pass after three thousand years. God's retribution had come full circle, and His promise to Solomon was fulfilled. Now the fire of hope may also be rekindled among the *Jinn*. The wonderment of His design dazzled my heart, and I said a silent prayer of thanksgiving for God's mercy on men and *Jinn* alike!

"Love covereth all sins," the Master said, reading my heart once again.

"You've quoted Proverbs," Professor Freeman said, "which King Solomon is said to have written in the wisdom of old age." He looked at his daughter and sighed. "This is beyond the knowledge of human science."

"Not so," the Master said. "The physical evolution of man and the universe runs parallel to a spiritual evolution, and the strands twist around each other like the braids of a rope. One can be explained by science, the other is incomprehensible, except to the science of the heart."

"Does the ring of King Solomon still abide then, as he wrote in his own blood?" the Professor asked.

"It does," said Ornias.

"Then I wish I had it now," Rebecca interrupted, "if only to command that damned wind to stop its howling. I can hear its echo in my mind even now."

"It would do you no good," the Master said. "The ring does not bestow power. It brings forth the truth of God within its bearer. Solomon, when God was with him and his wisdom still prevailed over his arrogance, brought the world under his sway with it, but it cannot alter by even an *aleph* the word of God."

"The word of God?" Rebecca asked. "What do you mean?"

"Never has the wind lessened since it's beginning," answered Ornias, "and may not till world's ending. The wings that imprison our fire will not yield to any but the Cause of all winds."

"Wings? What are you talking about?" Rebecca insisted.

"Do you not hear them, *Azza* and *Azzael*? Ever are they condemned to struggle against their chains, and ever do their great wings beat furiously in their torment. The *Jinn* are held captive by their fury, lest the fire of our lives be extinguished."

"*Azza* and *Azzael?*" Professor Freeman was astonished. "You mean the fallen angels? Their legend is in the *Zohar!*"

"Yes," said the Master. "And the truth of that legend lies at the foot of the Mountains of Darkness. There they are fettered in iron chains, and bands of iron hold them fast."

"And they can't free themselves? Angels?" Rebecca asked, wonder and pity in her voice.

The Master shook his head. "Their fetters are made of the iron of God's will, forged in the fire of His wrath. No power but His, who cast them down, can free their bonds and raise them up."

"Alas, they share our fate!" said Ornias.

"And your hope also," said the Master. "Who but Love shall

210

allay the divine Wrath? Who but Grace shall open the eyes? Verily, *'God's mercy precedeth His wrath!'* Thus it is written, and thus it has come to pass, and all His children may now walk the Path of Love if they will, men and *Jinn* and Angels cast down, though they trail their sixty thousand wings behind them."

"Allah!" Ali and Rami shouted together. *"Allah!"* I shouted with them. Rebecca burst into tears, and we called out to Him by many names, for the Master's revelation of God's infinite Love caused our souls to tremble with joy, to cry out with praise and gratitude; and the *zekr* of His name flowed from our hearts with every beat and with every breath, until the river of it swept both heart and breath into the Sea Without End. We wept as freely as children with the love that could not be contained, and it was a long time before any found words to speak. Verily, it seemed as if a Golden Age was upon us, wherein the awareness of God's Majesty and Beauty would be made manifest to all His children who dared to struggle and to love in His name.

And Professor Freeman's eyes, still wet with tears, were wild with the bewilderment of the boundless heart.

The Master looked upon his old friend and his voice was soft with understanding. "Ah, the intellect has gone crazy with love, and no longer fears its madness. You have come far, Shlomoh. Perhaps you were not my worst student."

The Professor could only laugh and shake his head. We laughed with him and Rebecca held his hand tightly.

The Master seemed about to say something more, but sighed instead and looked at Ornias. "The gates are open once again," he said.

"Not for long," replied the *Jinni*.

"Come then, all of you. We must go now, and quickly." The Master said, springing to his feet. We barely had time to gather our things before he hurried us down the steps and out of the palace. We soon were far up the marble road, the wind roaring around us as we ran. I imagined I could hear the *Jinn* whisper under its breath; and I looked back to see the lights of the columns blazing behind us in farewell.

Before the great open doorway of the circular structure we halted to take one last look at the land of the *Jinn*. All of fabled *Jinnistan* lay stretched out before us; the towering pinnacles of the city rising like stalagmites amid the jagged mountains, the immense terraces jutting from them in a geometry beyond human thought, and countless fires illuminating the night like torches. I wondered at the fate of the *Naqib*, and longed once more to see the light of the moon and stars. *And the sun, the sun!*

"Quickly now, or our fate will be the same," the Master shouted. He was already standing beside the burning pool with the *Naqib* and Ornias beside him, and Baalzeboul also, towering above them all. We hurried to them, but the sight of the burning pool made my heart sink. I knew how we must return.

The Master laughed at my forlorn look, and reaching inside his robe, brought out a leather waterskin.

"Here is a bottle cured in smoke," he said. "A gift of the Tuareg."

Ornias bowed to the *Naqib*. "Worthy is the gift and the giver. Alas, my own gifts I have left behind."

Baalzeboul sighed from his great height. "Would that I had any gifts to offer that were worthy of your deeds."

"Strive to the Truth," replied the Master. "And be steadfast.

There is no greater deed or gift." And with that he uncorked the bottle and poured its water onto the flames.

From what source he had filled the skin I knew at once. The flames did not sputter, but rose dancing merrily to greet it, and gladly were they consumed. Ornias and Baalzeboul watched intently as the small waterskin quenched the flames and filled the large pool with the purest of waters. I thought we would be plunged into darkness, but the water sparkled with a light of its own.

"Loaves and fishes! A miracle!" The Professor exclaimed.

The Master laughed. "No, not a miracle. The water of the Ocean of Love expands like the heart, without limit. Come now and cleanse yourselves. Such ablutions you will not make again in this life." He instructed us to gather around the pool and dip our faces into the water.

Ali and Rami did so at once, and Captain Simach and Rebecca after them. But Professor Freeman and I stared into the still water as if we were in a trance. We cast no reflection.

The Master did not wait. "Drop, wave, and bubble, all are one," he said, and pushed our heads under. The water filled my eyes and ears and mouth, its living presence expanding through me like a breath, suffusing every limb, every cell, until I felt my consciousness unfold like wings of light and fly gladly into the sun.

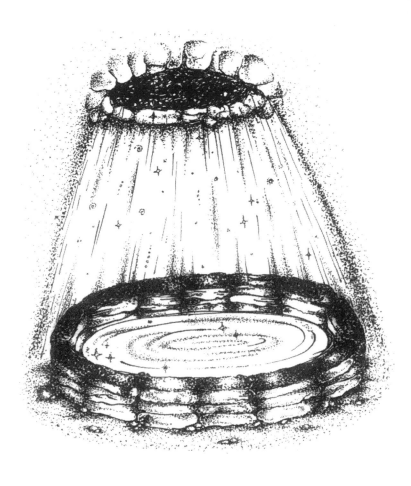

Epilogue

Alas, O ignorant one:
at the day of death
this will be proved;
A dream was what we saw,
what we heard, a tale.
—the *Urdu Diwan*
of Khwaja Mir Dard

Master of the Jinn

If you melt your soul in the fire of Love,
You will find Love to be the alchemy of your soul.

You will pass beyond the narrow straits of dimension,
And see the immensity of the dominion of nowhere.

That which your ear has not heard, you will hear;
That which your eye has not seen, you will see.
—Hatif Isphahani

I woke in my own room in the Master's house, in my own bed, stretching slowly out of sleep and into that sunlight I thought was a dream, feeling as refreshed as I have ever felt in my life. Once again I heard the old rooster crow his greeting to the dawn, and again the song of many birds rose in chorus to his call.

I sat up to find myself fully dressed, still wrapped in the blue Tuareg cloak given to me long ago, and laughed.

"Long may you live, old bird," I shouted, springing to the window. I could not help it. My heart could not contain its joy.

I had done my ablutions in the pure waters of Love and had been washed clean of doubt and fear. I had seen the circle close, and borne witness to the truth with the awareness of life. I laughed again with a clear heart and said my prayers while the birds sang. In unceasing gratitude for God's love and mercy, I prostrated myself and prayed for His grace on the Master, and on all His servants, and for His mercy on all the children of the two realms, and on the new Shaykh of *Jinnistan*.

Afterwards I hurried downstairs to once again heat the water for the morning tea and to search for the Master. For my companions, I had no fear. I had seen the pure waters wash over them, and surely the water of that sea which touches every shore had also borne them home. The Master, however, had not said when he would return, and as I set kettle over flame, I realized that I did not truly know even my own *when*. We had journeyed out of time, through fire and deep water, and I had no idea what day it was in this world, or what year.

It did not matter. I wished only to find him and be in his company, for I had glimpsed within the heart of his loving-kindness a reflection of the Mystery, and understood at last the words of Rumi when he spoke of his own Master, Shams-e Tabrizi:

> *I was dead; I have come alive!*
> *I was weeping; now I am laughing!*
> *The fortune of love has arrived,*
> *and I have become everlasting fortune!*

Thus the *Qutb,* the pole of the world, attracted me like iron to the magnet. Without looking for him, I found him. The Master was in the garden among the birds, and they sang to him once more as he sat on the stone bench.

"Ah good, you are awake," he said. "Shlomeh is coming tonight to be initiated, and we must purchase rock candy and coffee for Rebecca."

"Master, when did you return?" I asked.

"The moment you saw me," he answered.

"But what day is this?"

"It is today. A Sufi lives ever in the present, O scholar," he said laughing.

"*Alhamdulillah!*" I said, laughing with him. He rose and I fell into step next to him as we walked to the market once again.

And again the merchants offered their wares for his blessings, and once more he bid them distribute their offerings to the poor. The coffee he insisted on paying for, however, and the rock candy.

And as before we returned through the Old City, past the Haram al-Sharif mosque, but there was no *faqir* telling fortunes on its steps.

"You will not see him again in this life," the Master said, looking straight ahead. "The boundary is sealed by waters impassable to his race, and the Gates of Heaven will not open again until the Last Day."

I nodded, but the thought saddened me. I had indeed gone on the long journey he had foretold, that dreaded vampire spirit of the *Jinn*, the best of guides and most worthy of companions. Would that I knew his full tale. I will miss him.

Upon our return we found the *khaniqah* already crowded, in the midst of preparations for the feast that night. The women were cooking and the men were busy cleaning the common rooms. They were delighted to see the Master and he visited with them briefly, drank the offered tea, and then excused himself to go visit with his daughters. They said nothing of our absence, of course, and asked no questions, but neither did they jest with me after he had gone.

"You look older," Mojdeh said, and I saw them glancing at each other.

I did not answer. When I finally ventured into the garden I was delighted to find Ali and Rami, Rebecca and Captain Simach waiting for me. The Master had passed this way and told them I would be along presently. I breathed a sigh of relief and embraced my brothers and sister. They had arrived while we were out shopping and Rebecca said her father would also be here soon. He had insisted on stopping at his office. We sat together and talked softly, like old comrades who had often shared the same fire and had no need of explanations.

They too had awoken in their own beds, they said, and Rebecca and Captain Simach were also wrapped in their Tuareg cloaks. We shook our heads in wonder. Two months had passed in the world, it seems, and we looked at each other and began to laugh. Our mirth was joyous and contagious. We laughed and talked and Captain Simach admonished us to please call him Aaron.

I glanced around to see if anyone could overhear us, but there was no one else in the garden. Many *darvishes* would ordinarily be tending the garden at this time of day, but they had afforded us a welcome privacy. Such was the way of understanding in the *khaniqah*. I mentioned it to my companions, but they were not surprised.

"We have changed and they see it," said Aaron.

"I was told I look older," I said.

"You do look older," Rebecca said.

"Almost old enough to shave," said Rami, and they all laughed.

Indeed, in the mirror of the heart we had grown beyond our childhood. When the Master and Professor Freeman came into the garden some time later, we were still talking and laughing.

"So, you have all returned from the lesser battle to the greater one," said the Master, motioning for us to remain seated.

"What is the greater battle, Master?" asked Rebecca as they sat with us.

"Struggle with the *nafs*. It is a battle that has no end."

Professor Freeman nodded, his eyes sparkling. He looked younger.

Only the Master was the same, constant as the sea.

"And now," he said, "before Shlomeh is initiated, there is one deed left undone."

He turned to reach behind the old tree and brought forth the intricately carved *kashkul* the *faqir* had carried. I had not seen it since he had first appeared in the garden.

"Here are the gifts left behind, two within and one without, and three already given," said the Master. "The *kashkul* itself he gives to the *khaniqah*, and three gifts he has already given, and his words with them."

He then took two objects out of the *kashkul* and handed one of them to me, a small rectangular object wrapped in rough linen, tied with old twine.

"For the scholar, words," he said.

He then handed Professor Freeman a small, worn leather pouch, saying "For the seeker, the sought."

Three gifts already given?

I looked at the others in amazement. How much had I missed, constantly scribbling? I untied the twine and unwrapped the linen. It was a book of words indeed—a journal, perhaps. I turned to the first page but could not decipher the strange Hebraic script. It appeared to be written in the same ancient language as the papyrus. I held it open for Professor Freeman to see.

"Yes, yes!" he said after a moment's examination. "*Canaanitish*

without a doubt. And it is recently written. The paper is yellowed, but the fibers have only begun to break down. The book itself cannot be more than forty or fifty years old."

He turned the pages carefully as I held the book. For some reason I could not let it go, and he made no attempt to take it.

"Incredible!" he exclaimed. "A history of some kind, I think! I would be delighted to translate it for you."

I closed the book carefully and looked at the Master.

"Yes," he said. "It is meant for both of you. But beware! This gift is not given lightly. The tale may also translate you."

I took a deep breath and rewrapped it, retying the twine. *I had wished to know his tale.* My eyes filled with tears at the thought of him, and at the discovery of another of his names: *Scribe.*

"Come now, Shlomeh," the Master said. "Will you not also share your gift with us?"

Professor Freeman could not avert his gaze from the linen wrapped book, his attention absorbed in the secrets it might contain. Absently he pulled open the leather drawstring of the old pouch and tipped its contents onto his open palm.

Slowly his eyes focused on it, and for a long moment he stared at it.

"By the living God," he whispered.

A small gold ring had fallen into his hand, set with a single, beautiful green stone, ground flat and cut in the form of a star.

The boy sat curled and frightened as the Rebbe stood over him like a great black spectre, reaching a scarred and knotted hand to lightly touch the boy's brow with his forefinger. Instantly the boy

221

relaxed. The touch was somehow soothing and straightening at once. The boy sat up, feeling clearheaded and unafraid.

"Do you know who King Solomon is?" the old man asked.

The boy nodded. "My momma told me. I was named after him. He was smart."

The old man nodded, well pleased, and the boy flushed, proud of his answer.

"Yes he was, smart and wise, and indeed you were named after him. And you are also very smart. But do you know what it means to be wise?"

The boy thought and thought, until his face was scrunched with the effort.

"No," he said at last.

The old man laughed softly at his expression.

"Well, being wise means only two things. It is like a recipe, like mixing flour and water to make matzos. It is remembering God, and then acting from the heart of that remembrance."

"Huh?"

"You don't understand, I know, so I will tell you a story to explain."

The boy settled back in the large chair and tucked his legs under him, then wrapped his arms around himself until he felt snug and warm and ready to listen, as if he were home in bed and momma was reading to him. He could still hear his parents in the hall, but he did not want to call out to them now. He was no longer afraid of the old man.

The Rebbe watched the boy and smiled to himself. "This is a story you will remember," he said.

"Is it a long story?"

"Yes," the Rebbe said. "A very long story. But I only have time to tell you the first part. The rest you will learn later."

"What's it about?" the boy asked eagerly.

"It's about this," the Rebbe said, carefully taking a ring from his vest pocket. It was a shiny gold ring with a green jewel shaped like a star. "With a ring like this King Solomon could understand the language of birds, and he could control demons. Do you know what a demon is?"

The boy shook his head.

"It is like a Dybbuk."

"Oh!" the boy said. "A monster!"

"Yes," the Rebbe nodded.

"Where did King Solomon get the ring?" the boy asked.

"God gave it to him. Here, hold it." He dropped the ring carefully into the boy's small hand. It was large and heavy and the boy stared at it for a long time. The shiny gold and bright green jewel had him transfixed.

"Is it a magic ring?" the boy asked hopefully, his eyes wide.

"No," the Rebbe said. " The magic comes from the power of God within the one who wears it."

" What are you going to do with it?" the boy said, handing it back. He felt slightly disappointed.

"I will keep it safe until it is time to give it to someone else."

"Give it to who?"

"To whomever God wishes it to go to."

"Will God give it to me too, someday?"

"Perhaps He will," the old man said seriously, "when your heart is wise enough to know what to do with it."

I leaned in to get a closer look at the face of it, but Professor Freeman closed his hand and hid it from our view. I could not tell if the others had seen the ring at all. Only Rebecca was watching her father's reaction.

"And now," said the Master, looking up, " the gifts are given and the supper hour approaches. You are to be initiated beforehand, Shlomeh. Ishaq will bring you to me when you are ready." He rose and went into the *khaniqah*. Ali, Rami and Aaron followed at his signal.

Rebecca remained with her father as I explained the ceremony of initiation and its symbolic meanings. He had not raised his head, however, and I began to wonder if he was listening. His hand was still closed.

". . . And we have the rock candy. But if you need to go buy a –"

"Call me Solomon, please," he said abruptly, looking at his daughter. "And I don't need to go anywhere. I have a ring to give."

Thus it came to pass that Professor Solomon Freeman became initiated as a *darvish*, with feasting and music and the joyous clapping of hands. And the sound of Ali's *ney*, which had also been through fire and pure water, lifted our hearts to the realm where fire and water mingle, singing His praise.

After the initiation and a delicious dinner, we sat once more in the garden as the Master spoke.

"Know, O *darvish*, that love is the foundation and principle of the way to God, and that all states and stations are stages of love, which is not destructible so long as the Way itself remains in existence.

"Thus, it is written by Amr ibn Uthman Makki in the ancient

text, *Kitab-I Mahabbat*, the Book of Love, that God created the soul seven thousand years before the bodies, and kept it in the station of proximity. And He created the spirit seven thousand years before the soul and kept it in the degree of intimacy. And He created the heart seven thousand years before the spirit and kept it in the degree of union; and He revealed the epiphany of His beauty to the heart three hundred and sixty times every day, and bestowed on it three hundred and sixty looks of grace. And He caused the spirit to hear the true word of love, and manifested three hundred and sixty favors of intimacy to the soul.

"And so it was that when God had them survey the universe He had created, they saw nothing more precious than themselves, and were filled with pride and vanity.

"Thus God subjected them to probation; He imprisoned the heart and the spirit in the soul and the soul in the body. Then he mingled reason with them, and each of them began to seek its original station. The body prostrated itself in prayer, and the soul attained to love, the spirit arrived at proximity to God, and the heart found rest in union with Him."

The Master paused to light his pipe, his eyes searching our expectant faces as the white smoke curled above him. "Do not ask for explanations. Love cannot be explained. The explanation of love is not love, because love is beyond mere words. Indeed, if the whole world wished to attract love, they could not; and if they made the utmost efforts to repel it, they could not. For love is a Divine gift. It cannot be acquired, nor can it be fought."

Many sighed with longing at the Master's words, yet my heart felt only joy. And as the *darvishes* left that night, we embraced each other as fellow travelers, as heart companions, and as brothers and sisters.

Aaron and Rebecca did not look at each other during the Master's oration, nor afterwards when the last of the tea and sweets were cleared away. But they lingered near each other until the others had left, and I could see that, indeed, no explanations were necessary.

At last she kissed her father as he sat by himself. He was to spend the night in the *khaniqah* and begin his contemplations as a *darvish*. I walked with the Master as he accompanied them to the courtyard gate. They were loath to depart and stood in conversation for a time, but finally I kissed them both and they bowed to the Master, their hands over their hearts in farewell.

We watched them together as they walked down the path to the road beyond. The fields were wet from a late evening rain, and when the moon came out the freshness was still there. They walked hand in hand and sometimes a cloud would cover the moon.

When they had reached the road, the Master closed the gate and laughed softly. "The urge to love is a caress from heaven," he said.

As we walked toward the house he stopped to look at the night. The moon was perfectly full and the stars seemed near and brilliant. He reached into the pocket of his robe and withdrew a closed hand. Slowly he opened it and I saw that a brown moth lay in his palm, motionless and seemingly dead. He stroked it gently with his forefinger and blew softly on it. The wings began to stir, then flutter, and he raised his hand to the sky and set it flying. I saw it turn and twist in the wind, obeying an inner rhythm known only to its kind, though its course did not waver. Ever higher and higher it flew until it left my sight, and I knew that it was flying toward the night lamp of the world, and toward the light of its Beloved.

Acknowledgments

With unending gratitude, I thank the following people for their good counsel, support, inspiration, generosity and love:

Mr. Hasan Koshani, Mr. Leon Tiraspolsky, Ali Jamnia, Mojdeh Bayat, Maryann Lewis, Barbara Vaughan, Patricia Sweeney, and, always, Matthew and Rebecca.

Glossary of Terms

Adab – The courtesy, etiquette and manners of the Sufi Path.

Aether – A philosophical term for a substance that fills all space.

Ahaggar – A Large plateau or mountain region in the central Sahara.

Aleph – The first letter of the Hebrew and other Semitic languages.

Al-Muazzim – A Sorcerer; one who by black arts may command evil spirits to do his bidding.

Alhamdulillah – Arabic, meaning "All praise is God's (alone).

Allahu Akbar – Arabic, meaning "God is Great."

Amenukal – A Tuareg headman's title, meaning, "drum chief."

Asmodeus – A *Jinni* who professed the Hebrew faith and observed the Torah.

Awliya – Arabic, meaning "The friends of God."

Azazel – The Jinn taken in by the angels; who became Iblis (Satan) and was cast out of heaven when he refused to bow down to Adam at God's command.

Azrael – The Angel of Death. Azza,

Azzael – Two fallen Angels who, according to the Zohar, are chained near the Mountains of Darkness.

Baalzeboul – The ancient name given to the Lord of the *Jinn*.

Baraka – Blessing or Divine grace.

Barchan – A moving, crescent-shaped sand dune.

Benaiah – One of King David's warriors, faithful in David's old age to King Solomon, who was also said to be exceedingly fair of face.

Bismillah – Arabic, meaning, "In the name of Allah."

Bulla – A round, flat object used as a seal.

Canaanitish – The most archaic known form of the Hebrew alphabet.

Daf (s) – A shallow goatskin covered frame drum, played by hand.

Darvish – (or dervish). A disciple of a Sufi Master.

Dhu'l-Nun, the Egyptian – Dhu'l Nun Misri, the great Egyptian Sufi master (798-856 C.E.) is said to have been able to read hieroglyphics, and to possess a magic ring.

Dinar – A Middle-Eastern form of currency.

Envy – A *Jinni* with all the limbs of a man but without a head.

Erg – The true desert; a vast area of sand and dunes.

Faqir – Literally, poor one; in Sufi terms, one who lives in spiritual poverty, who is attached to nothing and wants nothing but God.

Gandura – A blue cloak worn by Tuareg tribesmen.

Garmi – Persian: a hot quality of food, not in temperature, but in the effect on the body.

Ghul – Shape-shifting Jinn, said to inhabit tombs and graveyards. Origin of Ghoul.

Golmos – A hollow, hard reed pen used for writing on papyrus in Biblical times.

Gomeh – The plant from which papyrus is made.

Guelta – A large, sandy rock-pool, found throughout the Sahara.

Haadi – One of the 99 names of God, al-Haadi means "the Guide."

Hajj – The Islamic pilgrimage to Mecca.

Iahar Halibanon – Hebrew, literally the Forest of Lebanon; an ancient name for King Solomon's palace.

Iblis – The name for Satan in the Koran, probably from the Arabic word *balasa*, which means, "he despaired," i.e., he despaired of the mercy of Allah.

Ifrit – Diabolical, evil Jinn.

Imam – Leader in Arabic. The term is generally applied to religious leaders. Also the 12 infallible and noble Imams, the descendants of Muhammad

Iman – Faith and trust in Allah.

Janannam – Arabic name for Hell.

Jasus el-Qulub – Literally, the Spy of Hearts; one who has the ability to read hearts and minds.

Jeroboam – King of northern Israel and ten of the twelve tribes, after Solomon's death split the kingdom. Rehoboam, Solomon's son, ruled the remaining two tribes.

Jinn – Spiritual beings created from fire that inhabit the world and are required to follow the orders of Allah and are accountable for their deeds. The word Jinn in Arabic means hidden, which indicates that they are invisible creatures.

Jinni – Singular form of *Jinn*.

Jinnistan – Literally, the land of the *Jinn*.

Joseph – Prophet in the Bible and Koran, known for his beauty and wisdom.

Kemi'a – A Biblical talisman, usually a written invocation carried to ward off evil.

Khaniqah – Persian, meaning the house of a Sufi order.

La, Scroll of – A fabled scroll in which is written the name of all those who have been disobedient to Allah.

La illaha illa Allah – Arabic for "There is no God, but God." Part of the Shahada, and often used as a zekr, it means: "There is no lord worthy of worship except Allah."

Luz – Mythical city where death cannot enter.

Mazel – Yiddish for luck, or good luck.

Modougou – Leader or boss of a caravan.

Mohasebeh – The balancing of accounts, in which a newly initiated darvish meditates on his past deeds.

Mossad – Israeli counterpart to America's CIA; foreign Intelligence service.

Muezzin – The one who calls Muslims to prayer five times a day, usually from the minaret of the local mosque by crying out the Call to Prayer.

Nafs – The lower self or ego of humanity's animal nature, which must be overcome to achieve Gnosis, or Oneness with Allah.

Naqib – Singular of Nuquba, one of the three humans that support or can substitute for the Qutb.

Negev – A desert in southern Israel.

Ney – A Persian knotgrass reed.

Nimrod – In the Koran, an evil king who threw Abraham in the fire.

233

Nuquba – See *Naqib*.

Onoskelis – A *Jinni* with the shape and skin of a fair-hued woman.

Ornias – A *Jinni* with vampire-like fangs.

Pentalpha – Five pointed star used as a magical symbol.

Qalandar – A lone, wandering darvish.

Qutb – The person considered the magnetic Pole or spiritual zenith of the Age.

Rabdos – A ravenous, hound-like *Jinni*.

Rak'at – An individual unit of the Muslim prayer.

Rebbe – Yiddish form of the word Rabbi.

Reg – A desert of covered with stones and pebbles leading to the Erg, or true sand desert.

Ruh – The divine spirit within human beings.

Salaam – Arabic greeting meaning "peace."

Sama – Meditation to music or song.

Sardi – Persian; a cold quality of food, not in temperature, but in the effect on the body.

Shahada – The declaration of faith. A person must recite the Shahada to convert to Islam, i.e., "I testify that there is no God but Allah, and I testify that Muhammad is the Messenger of Allah."

Shaitanun – Satan

Shamir – Legendary green stone or gem said to help build and be part of the first Temple in Jerusalam. Also said to be the stone or gem set in the seal ring of King Solomon, by which he commanded the Jinn.

Shaykh – or Shaikh. (1) The leader of a town or village. (2) The head religious (Islamic) functionary in a town or region. (3) In Sufism, a spiritual master.

Siddiq – Designates a person of illuminated inner vision; one whose word is truth.

Si'lat – The obligatory prayers.

Spy of Hearts – See Jasus el-Qulub.

Sufi, Sufism – Sufism is a term that designates Islam's mystical component. A Sufi is one who practices Sufism

Sufreh – (also sofreh) a white dining cloth spread on the floor or ground.

Tadmor – Mythical city built by King Solomon for the Queen of Sheba.

Tamashek – (or Tamajeg) The spoken Tuareg language. There is no written form.

Tar – A plucked string instrument formed of two bowls and shaped like a figure eight.

Tariqat – Mystical good conduct and worship that denotes the Sufi path.

Taslim – Arabic, literally meaning, "I gladly accept."

Tattala – Yiddish for little boy.

Tephros – A *Jinni*, called the demon of the Ashes.

Tombeck – (or Tonbeck); a goblet drum.

Tuareg – A term used to identify numerous diverse groups of people in Saharan Africa who share a common language and a common history.

Vizir – Principle advisor to the King or Sultan.

Wadi – A desert gully or ravine.

Wali – An Islamic term for saint. Also a legal guardian; a friend or protector.

Zadok – The High Priest of the first Temple during the reign of King Solomon.

Zekr – Literally, remembrance; in Sufism, the word or phrase given in secret to a darvish (or dervish) that he repeats with each breath, until the word flows into the heart, and each breath becomes a prayer and supplication.

Zohar – The Sefar Zohar, or "Book of Splendour," is a series of reputedly authoritative books on Kabbalistic teachings.

Zulaikha – Described in the Koran as the "most beautiful of stories," Jami's poetic romance of Yusuf (Joseph) and Zulaikha explores the theme of erotic and Divine love.

27434564R00128

Made in the USA
Lexington, KY
12 November 2013